The Rockingdown
Mystery

The Rockingdown Mystery

ENID BLYTON

Illustrated by Eric Rowe

AWARD PUBLICATIONS LIMITED

For further information on Enid Blyton
please contact www.blyton.com

ISBN 1-84135-175-X

Text copyright The Enid Blyton Company
Illustrations copyright © 2003 Award Publications Limited

Enid Blyton's signature is a trademark of
The Enid Blyton Company

This edition published by permission of
The Enid Blyton Company

First published 1949 by William Collins Sons & Co. Ltd
This edition first published 2003
2nd impression 2004

Published by Award Publications Limited,
27 Longford Street, London NW1 3DZ

Printed in India

Contents

1

The Beginning of the Holidays

"Hello, Roger!"

"Hello, Diana! Had a good term?"

The boy and girl grinned at one another, half-shy as they always were when they met again at the end of the school term. They were brother and sister, and rather alike to look at – sturdy, dark-haired, with determined chins and wide smiles.

"My train came in twenty minutes before yours," said Roger. "Bit of luck, breaking up on the same day – we usually don't. I waited about for you. Now we've got to wait for Miss Pepper."

Diana groaned. She dragged her overnight bag, her tennis racket and a large brown parcel along with her. Roger had a racket and a case too.

"These aren't going to be very nice hols," said Diana, "with Mummy and Daddy away, and us poked down in the country somewhere with Miss Pepper. Whatever made Mummy ask her to look after us?

Why couldn't we have gone to Auntie Pam?"

"Because her kids have got chicken-pox," said Roger. "Miss Pepper isn't so bad, really – I mean she does understand how hungry we always are, and she does know we like things like sausages and salad and cold meat and potatoes in their jackets and ice cream and lemonade . . ."

"Oh, don't go on – you make me feel hungry already," said Diana. "What are the plans for today, Roger? I only know you were going to meet me and then we were to wait for Miss Pepper somewhere."

"I had a letter from Dad yesterday," said Roger, as they pushed their way through the crowds on the platform. "He and Mum fly to America today. They had fixed up for us to go to Aunt Pam, but the chicken-pox knocked that on the head, so Mum phoned Miss Pepper and got her to fix up to spend the hols with us, and we're to go to a little cottage somewhere that Dad managed to get hold of in Rockingdown – goodness knows where that is!"

"Where we're to moulder all the hols, I suppose," said Diana, sulkily. "I think it's too bad."

"Well, there's a riding-school not far off and we can ride," said Roger, "and I believe there's a river near. We might get a boat. And it's good country all round Rockingdown for birds and flowers."

"All very nice for you because you're so mad on nature," said Diana. "I shall feel buried alive – no tennis, no parties – and I suppose that horrid little Snubby is coming too."

"Of course," said Roger, digging somebody hard with his tennis racket. "Oh, sorry! Did I hurt you? Do let's get out of this awful crowd, Di. We seem to be going round and round in it."

"We've got into one that's rushing for a train," said Diana. "Let them go by, for goodness sake. Look, here's a seat – let's sit down for a bit. When do we meet Miss Pepper?"

"Not for twenty-four minutes," said Roger, looking at the station clock. "Shall we go and see if we can get an ice cream somewhere nearby?"

Diana immediately got up from her seat. "Oh, yes – what a brainwave! Look, there's the exit. There'll be a tea shop or something nearby. We'll get ices there."

Over the ice creams the chatter went on.

"You said Snubby was coming, didn't you?" said Diana as she ate her strawberry ice. "Little pest!"

"Well, he hasn't got any parents," said Roger. "That's pretty awful, you know, Di. He gets kicked about from one aunt to another, poor kid, and he likes coming to us better than anywhere else. He's not so bad, if only he wouldn't play the fool so much."

"Just our luck to have an idiotic cousin with an idiotic dog," said Diana.

"Oh, I like Loony," said Roger at once. "He is quite potty, of course, but he's a lovely spaniel, he really is! Loony's a wonderful name for him – he's an absolute lunatic, but honestly he's great, the things he does. I bet he plays Miss Pepper up!"

"Yes, he'll go off with all her shoes and hide them under a bush, and fight her Sunday hat, and get himself cleverly locked up in the larder," said Diana. "What about another ice?"

"If Snubby was more our age, it wouldn't be so bad," said Roger. "After all, I'm fourteen and you're thirteen and he's only eleven – quite a baby."

"Well, he doesn't behave like one," said Diana, beginning on her second ice. "He behaves like a horrible little imp or goblin or something, always up to mischief of some sort, and thinking he can tag along with us. Oh dear – what with Miss Pepper and Snubby these hols look as if they'll be awful."

"Heavens, look at the time," said Roger. "We shall miss Miss Pepper if we don't look out. I must get the bill and we'll go."

The girl brought him the bill, and he got up with Diana to go to the desk and pay.

As they were going out of the door Roger glanced at Diana's hands. "Idiot! You've left your racket and bag at the table. I knew you would. You always do! It's a marvel to me you ever manage to bring anything home safely!"

"Rats!" said Diana, and went back to get her things, knocking over a chair in her impatience. Roger waited for her patiently, a grin on his good-looking face. Harum-scarum, untidy, impatient Di! He laughed at her, kept her in order, and was very fond of her indeed. He was fond of his cousin too, with his impudence, sense of fun, and his habit of doing the most surprising and annoying things.

Both Diana and Snubby would have to be kept in order these holidays, Roger was certain. Diana was cross and disappointed at being sent off with Miss Pepper to some place she had never heard of – she would be annoying and perhaps sulky. Snubby would be more irritating still, because he wouldn't have Roger's father to jump on him and yell at him. He would have Miss Pepper, and Snubby hadn't much opinion of women.

Loony the dog was, of course, another problem, but a very nice problem indeed. He was a dog who only obeyed one person and that was Snubby. He had never out-grown his habit of chewing things, hiding them and burying them. He went mad quite regularly, racing up and down the stairs, in and out of every room, barking his head off with excitement, and thoroughly upsetting every grown-up within miles.

But he was so beautiful! Roger thought of the little black spaniel with his silky, shining coat, his long drooping ears that always went into his dinner dish, and his melting, mournful eyes. How lucky Snubby was to have a dog like that! Roger had often smacked Loony for being wicked, but he had never ceased to love him. He was glad that Loony was to share the holidays with them, even though it meant having his cousin Snubby too.

"We've got to meet Miss Pepper under the station clock," said Roger. "We've got a minute to spare. Look – isn't that her?"

It was. The children took a good look at their mother's old governess as they hurried up to her. She was tall, thin, trim, with straight grey hair brushed back under a small black hat. Her eyes behind their glasses were sharp and twinkling. She had a very nice smile as she saw the children hurrying up to her.

"Roger! Diana! Here you are at last – and punctual to the minute too. It's a year since I saw you, but you haven't changed a scrap."

She kissed Diana and shook hands with Roger. "Now," she said, "we've a little time

before we have to leave for our train at another station – what about a couple of ices, or have you grown out of your liking for them?"

Roger and Diana brightened up at once. Neither of them said that they had just had two ices each. Diana nudged Roger and grinned. Miss Pepper certainly was good at remembering to provide ice cream and lemonade and the rest. She never failed in that.

"Now, I wonder where we can get ice creams without going too far," said Miss Pepper, looking round the station.

"Er – let me see – isn't there a little tea shop just outside the station?" said Roger.

"Yes, where they have lovely ices," said Diana. "Do you remember the way, Roger?"

Roger did, of course, and promptly led the way back to the little tea shop they had left only a few minutes before. Miss Pepper's eyes twinkled. She wondered how many ices the two had already had while waiting for her.

Roger led his sister and Miss Pepper to a different table this time. He didn't want the girl to make some remark that would give them away. They ordered ice creams.

"When is Snubby coming?" asked Diana.

"By train tomorrow," said Miss Pepper. "With Loony, I fear. I don't like dogs, as you know, and I like Loony even less than most dogs. It means I shall have to lock up all my slippers and hats and gloves. I never knew such a dog for smelling out things! Never! Last time I stayed with your mother, Roger, I began to think that Loony could undo suitcases, because the things I had put in disappeared regularly and I always found Loony with them sooner or later."

"I expect Snubby had something to do with that," said Roger. "He was awful those hols you were there, Miss Pepper. As loony as his dog."

"Well, I hope Mr Young will be able to keep Snubby in order," said Miss Pepper.

There was a sudden startled silence. Roger and Diana looked at Miss Pepper in alarm.

"Mr Young," said Roger. "What's he coming for?"

"To coach you all," said Miss Pepper, in surprise. "Didn't you know? I expect you'll get a letter soon, if you haven't heard. Your father rang up your schools, you know, to find out what kind of a report you both had, because he knew he wouldn't get it before he left for America – and you've got to have tutoring in Latin and maths, Roger, and you in French and English, Diana."

"Well!" said both children together. "How absolutely foul!"

"Oh, no," said Miss Pepper. "Mr Young is very nice – and a very good tutor. You've had him before."

"He's as dry as dust," Diana said angrily.

"Oh, I do think it's hateful – holidays without Mummy and Daddy, at a place we don't know anything about, with Mr Young and lessons – and—"

"Shut up, Di," said Roger, afraid that his angry sister would say something about Miss Pepper too. "You know we missed part of the Easter term because we were ill – we're behind in a good many things. I meant to do some work anyhow these hols."

"Yes – but Mr Young – with his beard and his sniffs and his 'My dear young lady!'" cried Diana. "I hate him. I'll jolly well write and tell Daddy what I think of him for—"

"That's enough Diana," said Miss Pepper in a sharp voice.

"Is Snubby having tutoring too?" asked Roger, kicking the furious Diana under the table to make her stop working herself into a rage.

"Yes. Unfortunately he had a very bad report from his headmaster," said Miss Pepper.

"That's nothing new," growled Diana. "And I ask you – can Mr Young do anything at all with Snubby? Snubby will lead him a frightful dance."

"Shall we have another ice?" said Miss Pepper, looking at her watch. "We've just time. Or do you feel too upset to have another?"

They certainly didn't feel too upset to have another ice cream and a lemonade on top of it. Roger began to talk cheerfully about the happenings of last term, and Diana gloomed over her ice for a minute or two and then cheered up too. After all, it was holidays – and it would be fun to explore a new place, and there would be riding and perhaps boating. Things might be worse!

"Time to go," said Miss Pepper. "We're having lunch on the train. I hope you'll enjoy that. We shall be at Rockingdown by teatime. Well, come along – and cheer up, Diana dear, I expect you'll enjoy the holidays just as much as you usually do!"

2

Rockingdown Cottage

Rockingdown Village was a tiny little place with a butcher's shop, a baker's and a general store, and plenty of farms and cottages around. The church tower showed above the trees, and the church bell could be heard quite clearly in the cottage where the children were to stay for the holidays.

This proved to be a very exciting little place. "It's more than a cottage," said Diana approvingly. "It's a nice old house, with lots of rooms."

"It used to belong to a big mansion about half a mile off – this cottage is actually in the grounds of the mansion," said Miss Pepper. "It was what is called the Dower House."

"What's that?" asked Diana.

"It was a house set aside for the mistress of the big mansion when her husband died and her son and his wife came to take over the mansion," said Miss Pepper. "She was then called the dowager mother, and came to live here, in this house, with her own servants."

"It's very old, isn't it?" said Diana, looking at the oak panelling of the dining-room in which they were having tea. "And I like the wide staircase – and the tiny little back staircase that winds up from the kitchen. We could have brilliant games of hide-and-seek here."

"I like my bedroom," said Roger. "It's got a ceiling that slants almost to the floor, and I've had to break away strands of ivy across one of the windows, Miss Pepper, it was so overgrown!"

"And I like the way the floor goes up and down," said Diana. "And the funny little steps down to this dining-room and up to the kitchen."

They were just what Miss Pepper didn't like. She was rather short-sighted, and in this old house she seemed to stumble everywhere. Still, no doubt she would get used to it!

"This tea is great," said Roger approvingly. "Did you make the scones, Miss Pepper?"

"Dear me, no – I'm afraid I'm no cook," said Miss Pepper. "Mrs Round made them. She's a village woman who comes in each day to do the cleaning and the cooking."

"Is she like her name?" said Diana at once. Miss Pepper considered.

"Well, yes," she said. "She is rather plumpish and her face certainly is very round. Yes – Mrs Round seems a good name for her."

The children were going to explore the house after they had had tea – and a very good tea it was, with home-made jam, home-produced honey, scones and a big fruit cake.

"This is the kind of fruit cake I like," said Diana, as she took a third slice. "You don't have to look and see if you've got any fruit in your slice – there's plenty all over the cake."

"You're a pig, Di," said Roger.

"People are always pigs at your age," said Miss Pepper. "Some are worse than others, of course."

"Am I a worse pig?" demanded Diana.

"Sometimes," said Miss Pepper, her eyes twinkling behind their glasses. Roger roared at Diana's indignant face.

"Miss Pepper, Di can eat a whole tin of condensed milk by herself," he began, and got a kick under the table.

"So could I, once," said Miss Pepper surprisingly. The children stared at her. It was quite impossible to imagine the thin, prim Miss Pepper ever having been greedy enough to devour a whole tin of condensed milk by herself.

"Go on, now, finish your tea," said Miss

Pepper. "I want to do your unpacking."

They explored while Miss Pepper unpacked their school trunks, exclaiming over the dirty clothes, and looking with horror at the rents and tears in most of Diana's things. Anyone would think that the girl spent all her time climbing thorn trees, judging by the state of her clothes. Miss Pepper thought of having to unpack Snubby's trunk the next day and shuddered. Really, children nowadays were quite impossible!

"Is the old mansion empty?" asked Roger that evening. "We saw it from a distance. There was no smoke coming from the chimneys. It looked a dead place."

"Yes, I believe it is," said Miss Pepper. "Roger, where are all the socks you took back to school with you? It says you took back eight pairs on this list, but I can only find one, very holey and dirty."

"I've got one pair on," said Roger helpfully. "That makes two."

"Miss Pepper, can we go and look over the mansion if it's empty?" asked Diana.

"No, I shouldn't think so," said Miss Pepper. "Diana, it says on your list that you took four blouses back to . . ."

Diana fled. It was dreadful the way grown-ups always put you through a cross-examination about clothes as soon as you got back from school. She and Roger rushed upstairs – and then tiptoed down the little back-stair and out into the garden.

Miss Pepper followed them upstairs in a moment or two, with another list of questions, but they had mysteriously disappeared. She looked round Diana's room and groaned. How could any girl make a perfectly neat room into such a terrible mess just one hour after she had taken possession of it?

Roger was pleased that night when the two of them went up to bed. "It's going to be a great place for birds, this," he told Diana. "And there are badgers here too – in these very grounds. One of these nights I'm going to get up and watch for them."

"Well, don't badger me to come with you!" said Diana, and shrieked as Roger aimed a punch at her for her pun.

"You sound like Snubby," he said. "He's always making silly puns and jokes. For goodness sake leave it to him!"

Their bedrooms were side by side under the slanting roof. Snubby's bedroom was across the landing, a tiny one looking to the back of the house, across the grounds. Miss Pepper slept on the first floor. Tucked away in another corner of the first floor were two other rooms.

"We'll have to meet Snubby tomorrow," said Roger, calling from his bedroom as he undressed. "And Loony."

"Yes. We'll walk over to the station," said

Diana, flinging all her clothes on the floor one by one, although she knew perfectly well she would have to get out of bed and pick them up as soon as Miss Pepper arrived to say goodnight. "It's only about two miles. I could do with a good long walk. We can bus back if Snubby's got a lot of things."

The next day was brilliantly fine. Snubby's train was due in at half past twelve.

"We'll go and meet him," said Roger to Miss Pepper. "You needn't come unless you want to, Miss Pepper. I expect there are lots of things you want to do."

They set off at twelve o'clock to walk to the station. They decided that the shortest way would be to go through the grounds of the old mansion. They were horrified to see how overgrown everything was. Even the paths were almost lost in the nettles and brambles that spread all round. Only one broad drive seemed to be at all well-kept, and that was now beginning to show signs of being covered with weeds.

"Funny," said Diana. "You'd think that whoever owned this place would want to keep it up decently, so that he could sell it at a good price, even if he didn't have any intention of living in it himself. How on earth are we going to get through these brambles? I'll scratch my legs to pieces."

Here and there, as they walked through the large grounds, they caught sight of the old mansion through gaps in the trees. It certainly looked a desolate place. Diana didn't like it.

"Well, I don't much feel as if I want to explore that," she said. "It would be full of spiders and creepy things and horrid noises and draughts from nowhere. A nasty, spooky place."

They were out of the grounds at last and came to the village. They stopped for an ice cream at the little general store.

"Ah – you're the new people in Rockingdown Cottage," said the old woman who served them. "That's a nice old place. I remember old Lady Rockingdown going down there when her son brought his wife home from Italy. Those were grand days – parties and balls and hunts and such goings-on! Now it's all dead and done with."

The children ate their ice creams and listened with interest. "Where did the family go, then?" asked Roger.

"Lady Rockingdown's son was killed in the Great War and his wife died of a broken heart," said the old woman, remembering. "The place went to a cousin, but he never lived there. He just let it. Then it was taken over in the last war, and some kind of secret work was done there – we never knew what. Now that's finished, of course, and the place has been empty ever since. Nobody wants it, it's so big and cumbersome. Ah – but it was a fine place once, and many's the time I've been up to it when my mother helped with a party!"

"We must go," said Roger to Diana, "else we shall be late for the train. Come on!"

He paid for the ices and they ran off to the station. They got there just as the train was coming in. They stood on the platform waiting for Snubby and Loony to appear from a carriage. Usually they both fell out together!

An old woman got down. A farmer and his wife appeared. But nobody else at all. The train gave itself a little shake, preparing to start off again. Roger ran all down it, looking into the carriages for Snubby. Had he fallen asleep?

There was no one in the carriages except another farmer and a young woman with a baby.

The guard blew his whistle and the train glided off importantly. There was no other train for two hours.

It took the children a little time to find this out, because there didn't seem to be anyone at the station. No one in the tiny booking office, no one in the stationmaster's room or in the waiting-room.

"Blow Snubby! He's missed the train," said Diana. "Just like him! He might have phoned to say so – then we needn't have walked all the way to meet him!"

They found a timetable that told them what trains there were. It took Roger a good ten minutes to discover that there were no more trains till the afternoon.

He looked at the station clock which now said a quarter past one. "We've wasted nearly an hour here," he said in disgust. "Messing about looking for Snubby and hunting for someone to ask about trains and trying to find out what the timetable says. Come on, let's go home. We'll catch the bus and perhaps we shan't be awfully late. Miss Pepper said she'd make lunch at one o'clock – we should be back by half past."

But there was no bus for an hour so they had to walk. The sun was hot and they were hungry and thirsty. Blow Snubby!

They arrived back at the cottage at two o'clock – and there, sitting at the table, looking very full indeed, was their cousin Snubby!

"Hello!" he said. "You *are* late! Whatever happened?"

3

Snubby – and Loony

Diana and Roger had no wish to fling themselves joyfully on Snubby; but Loony flung
himself on them so violently that he almost
knocked Diana over. He appeared from
under the table, barking madly, and threw
himself at them.

"Hey – wait a bit!" said Roger, very
pleased to see Loony. The spaniel licked him
lavishly, whining joyfully. Miss Pepper
looked crossly at them.

"Diana! Roger! You are very late."

"Well!" said Diana indignantly. "Snubby
wasn't on the train and we waited and
waited, and tried to find out when the next
train was. It wasn't our fault!"

"We've had lunch already," said Snubby.
"I was so hungry I couldn't wait."

"Sit down, Roger and Diana," said Miss
Pepper. "Snubby, call Loony to you, for
goodness sake!"

Roger and Diana sat down. Loony tore
back to Snubby and began to fawn on him

as if he too had been away for some time.

"Still the same old lunatic," said Diana, holding out her plate for some cold meat-pie. "Snubby, what happened to you?"

"I suppose you were late for the train, and missed Snubby and didn't see him or Loony on the road," said Miss Pepper. "I ought to have gone to meet him myself."

"They're not very observant," said Snubby, accepting another helping of tinned peaches and cream. "I mean I could walk right past them with Loony, under their noses, and they wouldn't see me."

Diana looked at him scornfully. "Don't be an idiot. You can't make out you passed us and we didn't see you."

"Well, what else could have happened?" said Miss Pepper. "Snubby, I will not have Loony fed at mealtimes. If you give him any more titbits I shall say he's to remain out of the room when we have a meal."

"He'd only scratch the door down," said Snubby. "As I said, my two cousins are not very observant, Miss Pepper. Fancy not even seeing Loony."

Loony jumped up in excitement whenever his name was mentioned. Miss Pepper made a resolve that she would never mention his name at all – only refer to him as "the dog". Oh dear, things were going to be twice as difficult with this mischievous boy and his excitable little dog.

"Snubby, you didn't come by that train," said Roger quietly. "What did you do? Go on, tell us or we'll never go to meet you again."

"I got out at the station four miles before Rockingdown," said Snubby. "The train had to wait three-quarters of an hour there for a connection so out I got, hopped on to a bus and here I was at a quarter to one! Easy!"

"Oh, Snubby!" said Miss Pepper. "Why couldn't you have said so before? It was so nice of your cousins to come and meet you – and all you did was to make them late for their lunch, and arrive cross and hot and hungry."

Diana glared at Snubby. "He's just the same horrid little boy," she said to Roger, speaking as if Snubby wasn't there. "Same old ginger hair, same old green eyes, same old snub nose, and same old cheek. I'm sure I don't know why we put up with him."

"Well, I put up with you," said Snubby, wrinkling his turned-up nose and grinning, so that his face appeared to be made of rubber, and his eyes almost disappeared under his sandy eyebrows. "Sorry to upset you, cousins. Honestly, I didn't know you were going to meet me. I'm not used to kind attentions of that sort from you. Are we, Loony?"

Loony leaped up madly and pawed violently at Snubby's knees, knocking his head against the table. He whined and yapped.

"Loony wants to go out," said Snubby, who used Loony as an excuse whenever he wanted to go wandering off by himself. "Can we go, Miss Pepper?"

"Yes," said Miss Pepper, thankful to be rid of them both. "Leave him outside in the garden when you come in again, and then go upstairs to help me unpack your trunk. It came this morning."

Diana and Roger finished their meal in peace. Roger grinned to himself. What an idiot Snubby was but it would certainly liven things up a bit to have him there – and Loony too. Diana glared at her peaches and cream. She wasn't pleased. She would rather have had Roger to herself. She knew that Snubby admired Roger and wanted to be with him, and this always made her want to push Snubby away.

Except for the fact that Snubby found an outsize beetle in the garden, which he insisted on displaying on the tea table, and that he had arrived with another boy's trunk instead of his own, things passed off peacefully the first day.

He and Loony thoroughly explored everywhere by themselves. Snubby hated being shown round. He liked to size things up for himself and go his own way. He was a most intelligent and sharp-witted boy, very clever at hiding his brains under a constant stream of tricks, jokes and general idiocies. He was adored by all the boys in his form and was their natural leader – but the despair of all the masters who seemed to vie with one another in making biting remarks about his work and character in his reports.

His jokes and tricks were endless. All his pocket money was spent on ice creams, chocolate, or the latest trick. It was Snubby who tried out all the trick pencils on the various masters: the pencil whose point wobbled because it was made of rubber; the one whose point disappeared inside the pencil as soon as the unsuspecting master tried to write; the pencil that could be nailed to the floor and couldn't be picked up.

It was Snubby who experimented with stink pills which, when thrown on the fire, at once gave out a smell like bad fish; and Snubby who climbed to the top of the school tower without falling. Everything was always Snubby – even when it really wasn't! But Snubby didn't mind. He accepted his punishments, rightful ones or wrongful, with pluck and resignation, and always owned up when tackled.

"A bad boy with a lot of good in him," said the headmaster. "It's a pity he has no parents. If he had he would behave better because he wouldn't like to let them down. He'll turn out all right – but in the meantime he's a pest."

Snubby was pleased with Rockingdown Cottage and the garden and grounds of the old mansion. He could make plenty of good hidy-holes in the grounds for Loony and himself. They could play all sorts of games to their hearts' content under the thick bushes, and up in the tall trees – because Loony didn't mind being dragged up trees by the scruff of the neck. In fact, he didn't mind where he went as long as he was with his beloved master. He had even been known to crouch in a smelly dustbin with Snubby for an hour while Snubby waited to play a trick on an unsuspecting delivery boy.

Snubby made his mind up to explore the old mansion. It would be locked and bolted and barred, but he'd get in somewhere all right. If Di and Roger would come too, that would be fun – if not, he'd go by himself. He hoped Roger would come, though. He would like to be in Roger's good books – Roger was okay. Diana was a nuisance – but then, in Snubby's opinion all girls were a nuisance. Always in the way.

It was a terrible shock to Snubby to hear that he was to have tutoring those holidays. Diana broke the news to him that night.

"You know you're to have lessons these hols, don't you, Snubby?" she said. "Mr Young's coming to coach you."

Snubby stared at her in horror. "I don't believe you," he said at last. "Nobody could do that to me – make me learn things in the summer hols! I've never heard of any such thing."

"Well, you'll have to believe it," said Diana. "Daddy's arranged it. Roger is to have tutoring in Latin and maths, I'm to be tutored in French and English."

"What am I to be tutored in?" Snubby said gloomily.

"Oh, I should think you need everything," said Diana. "I don't suppose you know your tables properly yet, do you, Snubby? And can you spell yet?"

"All right. I'll pay you back for that,"

said Snubby. "What about a worm or two under your pillow?"

"If you start doing that kind of babyish thing again I'll sit on you and bounce up and down till you cry for mercy," said Diana. "I'm much bigger than you are, baby-boy!"

This was quite true. Snubby was not big for his age and hadn't really begun to grow yet. Diana was a sturdy girl, and quite able to do what she threatened.

Loony appeared and rolled himself over and over on the floor. Snubby tickled him with his foot. The spaniel leaped up and fetched something from the hall. Diana gave a shriek.

"Oh – he's got my hairbrush. Snubby, get it from him. Quick!"

"Why? You never use it, do you?" said Snubby, neatly getting back at his cousin for her jibes of a minute or two ago. "What good is it to you? You might as well let Loony play with it."

The brush was rescued and Loony got a spank with it from Diana. He retired under the table, and looked at her mournfully with big brown eyes.

"Now you've hurt his feelings," said Snubby.

"I'd like to hurt a lot more of him than that," said Diana. "Now I shall have to wash this chewed-up brush. Blast Loony!"

"Blast everything!" said Snubby dismally. "Fancy – tutoring with Mr Young. I can't think of anything worse!"

4

Changed Plans

But after all Mr Young didn't come to tutor the three children. Two days later, when Roger, Diana and Snubby had put out their school books neatly on the study table, and had gloomily sharpened their pencils and found their pens, the telephone bell rang shrilly.

"I'll answer it, Miss Pepper, I'll answer it!" yelled Snubby, who adored answering the phone and pretending to be one of the grown-ups in the house. He rushed to answer.

The others listened, bored. Probably it was the butcher saying he couldn't deliver the meat, and one of them would have to fetch it.

"Yes. This is Rockingdown Cottage," they heard Snubby say. "Oh – who? Oh, Mrs Young. Oh, yes, certainly. Yes. I can give any message you like. Certainly. Dear, dear, how very, very sad. I'm so sorry to hear that. Well, well, to think how suddenly these things happen! And is he getting on all right? That's wonderful, isn't it? You have my deepest sympathy, Mrs Young – such a terrible time for you. Yes, yes, I'll give your message. Certainly. Goodbye."

By this time both Diana and Roger were out in the hall, amazed at Snubby's speech.

"What is it? What are you saying? Who on earth are you pretending to be, Snubby?" demanded Diana.

"Nobody. I'm just being polite and helpful," said Snubby, beaming. "I say – Mr Young's gone and got appendicitis and he's not coming! What do you think of that?"

The others stared at him. "Gosh – we couldn't think what you were doing, talking in that idiotic way over the phone!" said Diana.

"It wasn't idiotic. It was only like grown-ups talk," said Snubby. "I can tell you I felt very sorry for Mr Young – you know, having to go to hospital and everything."

"You didn't," said Roger. "You know you're always saying appendicitis is nothing, and telling us how you had it and enjoyed it. But I say – does this mean no tutoring then? Of course, it's upsetting for Mrs Young but it does solve a problem for us. We can enjoy ourselves now."

Loony was barking round their ankles, sensing their excitement. Miss Pepper came down the stairs.

"What's all the excitement about? Who was that on the telephone? I hope it wasn't the butcher again."

"No. It was Mrs Young," said Snubby. "Mr Young is in hospital with appendicitis, Miss Pepper. He's not coming to tutor us."

"Dear, dear! I am sorry for poor Mrs Young," said Miss Pepper in exactly the same voice that Snubby had used over the telephone. "Well – that does put us into a difficulty."

"Does it?" said Diana, astonished. "It seems to us that we've got out of one."

"Oh, dear me, no!" said Miss Pepper at once. "I shall get someone else to tutor you. I can't imagine who though. I shall have to go through my list of tutors. Snubby, stop Loony eating that rug. He's had more than half of it since he arrived and I should like a little bit left."

"He thinks it's a rabbit – it's a furry rug, you see," said Snubby.

"I don't care what he thinks it is," said Miss Pepper. "You heard what I said. Take Loony out of the hall at once. I'm getting tired of him already. He's run off with Mrs Round's hearthbrush and left it somewhere. He's been in the larder twice. He's pulled every mat into a heap on the landing. And if I catch him under my bed again he'll be in serious trouble," said poor Miss Pepper.

Loony suddenly sneezed and looked very

surprised at himself. He was always surprised when he sneezed. He sneezed again.

"Now what's the matter with him?" said Miss Pepper. "Sneezing all over the place."

"He's had too much pepper," said Snubby at once. "That's what it is – too much pepper – it's got up his nose. There's a lot of it about these days."

Miss Pepper looked at him coldly. "Don't be rude, Snubby," she said, and went into the dining-room. Roger roared and Snubby grinned.

"Let's all sneeze when Miss Pepper gets peppery," he said. "She'll stop telling us off then. Loony, clear out. You really will get into trouble if you go off with any more of Mrs Round's brushes. Besides, you're not to, anyway. She's nice."

Mrs Round appeared at this minute. She was certainly like her name and her face shone like the harvest moon, it was so red and round.

"That dog of yours," she began, "if he hasn't got my hearthbrush somewhere now! And if I chase him off with my broom what does he do but think I'm playing a game with him. Loony by name and loony by nature that dog is."

"What's for pudding today, Mrs Round?" asked Snubby, changing the subject in his clever way. "Are you going to make us one of your wonderful treacle puddings again?

Honestly, I wish you'd come and be cook at our school. The boys would cheer you every day."

Mrs Round beamed and patted the bun of hair at the back of her head. "Oh, go on with you now!" she said in her pleasant country voice. "You keep that dog of yours out of my kitchen, and I might make you pancakes with raspberry jam."

"Loony! Don't you dare go into Mrs Round's kitchen today," said Snubby sternly, and Loony wagged his little black tail. He crawled humbly on his tummy to Snubby and lay quite flat in front of him.

"All humbug," said Diana. "He's as good at pretending as you are, Snubby!"

Miss Pepper came out into the hall. "Are you still here?" she said to Loony, who promptly went out of the front door at top speed. She turned to the children. "I'm going to telephone one or two tutors I know to see if one is free to come. Go and clear away your books now. There certainly won't be any lessons today."

They cleared away their books thankfully. Miss Pepper was on the phone for some time and then came into the study. "It's no use," she said. "Everyone is either already fixed up, or is away. I'll have to put an advertisement in the newspapers."

"Oh, don't bother to do that, Miss Pepper," said Roger. "All this trouble for you! It's dreadful! I'm sure Dad wouldn't want you to bother like this."

"Then you think wrong, Roger," said Miss Pepper, and began to draft out an advertisement. It went off by the next post, much to the children's annoyance.

"Goodness knows who we'll get now," said Diana gloomily. "At least we knew Mr Young – and we know how to get him talking so that we didn't have to do much work ourselves."

For the next three days the children were quite free to do what they liked. They found the riding-school, and Miss Pepper arranged for one whole-day ride, and two hour-rides. That was fun. Loony was the only one who disapproved of it. He hated Snubby and the others to go off on horses, because sooner or later he couldn't keep up with them and dropped back. The stable dog, a big Airedale, kept up with the whole ride easily and was very scornful of the little spaniel.

They found the river and hired a boat. They could all swim like fishes, so Miss Pepper didn't worry about them on the river. They explored the countryside, and enjoyed looking for uncommon flowers, unusual birds and strange beetles. At least the two boys did; Diana didn't do much seeking for birds and flowers, she "mooned along" as the boys called it, enjoying the smells, the sounds and the sights of the countryside –

the smell of the meadow-sweet, the blue of the chicory, the little trill of the yellow-hammer and the blue flash of the kingfisher as he flew past them crying "tee-tee-tee".

On the third day Snubby roused the scorn of the others. Diana was sitting beside the bank of the river, watching for the king-fisher again. Roger was lying on his back with his arm over his eyes, listening to the high twitter of the swallows as they darted over the water, skimming the surface for flies.

Snubby was nowhere to be seen. He had crawled off to see if he could watch a few young rabbits who had unexpectedly come out to play in the daylight. Suddenly he came back.

"I say! Do you know what I've just seen?"

"A white butterfly," suggested Diana.

"A dandelion," said Roger, not moving.

"A monkey!" said Snubby. "Yes, go on, laugh. But I tell you it was a monkey!"

"Don't try and tell us one of your tall stories," said Roger. "We're not in the lower third with you."

"Look here – I tell you I *did* see a monkey," repeated Snubby. "It isn't a tall story. It was at the top of a tree and it swung itself down halfway, then saw me and disappeared. Loony didn't see it – but he certainly smelled it. I could see his nose twitching like anything."

Diana and Roger stopped listening. Snubby had too many marvels to tell – wonderful things always seemed to happen to him and this must be one of them! Diana shushed him.

"Shh! I think I can hear the kingfisher. He may come and sit on this branch."

"You are a disbelieving lot," said Snubby bitterly. "Here I come and tell you, absolutely solemnly and truthfully, that I've just seen a monkey, and all you do is talk about kingfishers."

Nobody said anything. Snubby sniffed scornfully. "All right – I'm going off by myself. And I shan't come back and tell you if I see a chimpanzee this time!"

He went off with Loony. Roger gave a gentle little snore – he was asleep. Diana sat with her chin on her knees, and was at last rewarded for her long wait. The kingfisher flashed down, sat on the branch just in front of her, and waited for a fish to swim along in the water beneath.

Snubby went gloomily through the wood behind. Loony trotted along at his heels, pondering over the inexplicable ways of rabbits that lived down holes too small for dogs to get into.

Then he stopped and growled deep down in his throat. "What's up?" said Snubby. "Oh – somebody coming? I can hear them now. Wish I had ears like yours, Loony, though how you hear at all with those big ears flapping over your ear-holes, I really don't know!"

Somebody came through the woods, whistling softly, and Loony growled again. Then Snubby saw the newcomer. He was a boy of about fourteen or fifteen, burnt very brown. His hair was corn-coloured and he had eyes so blue that they were quite startling to look at. They were set curiously wide apart and fringed with thick dark lashes. He had a very wide mouth that grinned in a friendly fashion at Snubby.

"Hello!" said the boy. "Have you seen a monkey?"

5

Barney and Miranda

That was the first time any of the three children saw the strange boy they were to know so well. Snubby stared at him, his brilliant, wide-set blue eyes and friendly grin. He liked this boy immensely, but he didn't know why.

"Lost your tongue?" said the boy. "Well, I've lost my monkey. Have you seen one anywhere?"

The boy did not talk quite like anyone Snubby had ever heard. He had a slight American twang, and yet he sounded foreign. Spanish – Italian – what could it be? Nor did he look English, for all his blue eyes and fair hair.

Snubby found his tongue. "Yes!" he said. "I have seen a monkey. I saw one about five minutes ago. I'll take you to where I saw him."

"Her," said the boy. "It's a she-monkey. She's called Miranda."

"Is she really yours?" said Snubby. "I've

always wanted a monkey. I've only got a dog."

"Lovely dog, though," said the boy, and he gave Loony a pat. Loony at once rolled over on his back and put all his legs into the air, doing a kind of bicycling movement upside down.

"Clever dog," said the boy. "Why don't you get him a little bicycle?" he said, turning to Snubby. "See how well he pedals upside down. Get a bike with four pedals and you could make a fortune out of him. The only bicycling dog in the world!"

"Do you really mean it?" said Snubby eagerly. He was ready to believe anything wonderful about Loony. The boy laughed.

"No. Course not. Come on, where's this tree? I must find Miranda – she's been gone an hour!"

Miranda was in the tree next to the one that Snubby had first seen her in. The boy gave his soft little whistle and the monkey leaped down like a squirrel, landing in his arms. He fondled her and scolded her.

"You know," said Snubby, trying to keep the excited Loony away from the monkey, "you know, I told my two cousins about the monkey and they absolutely refused to believe me. I suppose you wouldn't play a little trick on them for me?"

"If you like," said the boy, turning his blue eyes on Snubby with an amused look in them. "What do you want me to do?"

"Well – do you think you could make Miranda walk all round my cousins, or something like that, and then come back to you?" said Snubby eagerly. "Then I could go up and they'd tell me they'd seen the monkey too and I'd disbelieve them like they disbelieved me!"

"Not much of a trick," said the boy. "I'll tell Miranda to drop on them from the tree and leap off again. Give them a bit of a fright."

"Could you make her do that?" said Snubby.

"You bet!" said the boy. "Where are these cousins of yours? Come on – we'll liven them up a bit. We won't show ourselves, though."

They crept down towards the river. Snubby made Loony crouch down quietly. He pointed out Diana to the boy, and then Roger. The boy nodded. He said a few quiet words to the monkey who answered him in a funny little chattering voice and then sped up into the trees. The two boys watched. Loony looked most surprised to see the monkey disappear into the tree above him. Cats did that, but this creature didn't look or smell like a cat.

Miranda made her way to the tree immediately above Roger, who was lying asleep with his arm over his face. The monkey leaped down and then jumped full on top of Roger. Diana turned in astonishment, her eyes almost falling out of her head when she saw Miranda leaping down on Roger and then leaping up into the tree again and disappearing.

Roger woke with a start and sat up hurriedly. "What fell on me?" he said to Diana.

"A monkey," said Diana. "A little brown one."

"Oh, don't you start on about monkeys," said Roger crossly. "Anyone would think this place was full of monkeys the way you and Snubby go on about them."

"But, Roger – honestly, it *was* a monkey," said Diana.

"You and Snubby can go on telling me all day long that you keep seeing monkeys, but I shan't believe there's a monkey about even if I see one!" said Roger.

And at that very moment he saw Miranda! He saw her sitting on the strange boy's shoulder, as he came along with Snubby, both of them grinning widely.

Roger had to believe in the monkey then. He was astonished. "Is that your monkey?" he said to the boy. "Is it a pet?"

"Sure," said the boy. "Are you a pet, Miranda?"

Miranda chattered and put a little brown paw down the boy's neck. "Don't tickle," he said. "Shake hands with these people, and show how good your manners are."

Loony sat open-mouthed while Miranda gravely held out a little paw and allowed Roger, Diana and Snubby to shake it. The boy sat down beside them. Loony at once made a rush for Miranda. He was jealous.

Quick as lightning the monkey leaped off the boy's shoulder and on to Loony's back. She held on tightly and he couldn't get her off till he rolled on the ground. The children roared.

"Poor old Loony, nobody's ever tried to ride him before," said Diana. "What did you say her name was – Miranda? What a strange name for a monkey."

"Why?" said the boy. "I thought it was a mighty pretty name when I first read it, and it just suits Miranda – she's pretty too."

None of the three children thought that Miranda was pretty, though they all thought she was sweet and amusing. Still, they were used to people thinking their pets pretty and marvellous even though they mostly weren't.

"She's cute, isn't she?" said the boy, as Miranda began to turn head over heels very fast indeed. "She can do no end of tricks. Turn cartwheels, Miranda."

Miranda turned dozens of cartwheels, going over and over on hands and feet without stopping. Loony regarded her solemnly. No – this couldn't be a cat. No cat he had ever seen behaved like this.

"What's your name?" asked Roger, liking this strange boy just as much as Snubby did.

"Barney – short for Barnabas," said the boy.

"Where do you live?" asked Snubby.

The boy hesitated. "Nowhere at present," he said. "I'm just tramping around."

This was puzzling. "What do you mean? Are you on a hiking trip, or something?" asked Diana.

"You might call it that," said the boy.

"Well, where's your real home?" persisted Snubby. "You must have a home!"

"Don't pester Barney," sad Roger, seeing the boy hesitate again. "You're always so inquisitive, Snubby."

"It's all right," said Barney, and he rubbed Miranda's fur gently. "Actually I'm looking for my father."

This sounded odd. "Doesn't your mother know where he is?" demanded Snubby.

"My mother's dead," said Barney. "She died last year. I don't want to talk about that, see? I don't know much about her myself, or about myself either, but I'm trying to find out. My mother was in the show business – you know, travelling round in a circus, and attending fairs and things like that. She was wonderful with animals. I thought my father was dead – but just before she died my mother told me that she didn't think he was. He was an actor –

acted in Shakespeare plays, she said – and she ran away from him after she'd been married three months. He doesn't know anything about me."

"Don't tell us all this," said Roger awkwardly. "It's your own private business."

"I want to talk to somebody," said Barney, looking at them with his startling blue eyes. "But there's been no one to talk to. Well, when my mother died I felt sort of lonely, and I couldn't settle to anything. So I thought I'd go off on my own – with Miranda, of course – and see if I could find my father. I'd like to know there was somebody belonging to me, even if he turned out to be a disappointment."

"I haven't any father or mother," said Snubby. "But I'm lucky. I've heaps of other relations and they're jolly decent to me. I'd hate to have no one – only just Loony."

Diana couldn't imagine what things would be like without her mother. She was sorry for Barney. "What do you do for money, then?" she asked him.

"Oh, just scrounge around," said the boy. "I can always go to a circus or fair, you know, and earn some money there. There's not much I can't do. I've often been in the circus ring with Miranda here. I've just left the fair over at Northcotling. I'm at a loose end now, wandering about with Miranda. What I want to do is to get hold of some of

Shakespeare's plays and read them. I suppose you can't lend me any?"

Snubby couldn't imagine why anyone would want to borrow Shakespeare's plays. Diana tumbled to it at once.

"You want to know the plays that your father acts in – or used to act in!" she said. "You want to know the things he liked and the parts he could play!"

"That's right," said Barney, pleased. "I've only read one of them – about a storm and a shipwreck, it was. It's where I got Miranda's name from."

"Oh yes – *The Tempest*," said Roger. "That's quite a good one to start off with. Do you really want to read the plays? They'll be pretty difficult for you. If you really do, I'll lend you some."

"Thanks," said the boy. "Where do you live?"

"Over at Rockingdown Cottage," said Roger. "Do you know it?" Barney nodded.

"Where are you living just at present?" Diana said curiously. It seemed odd to think of somebody without a bed at night.

"Oh – in this weather I can sleep anywhere," said Barney. "Under a hedge, in a barn, even up a tree with Miranda so long as I tie myself on."

Diana glanced at her watch and gave an exclamation. "Do you know what the time is, boys? It's a quarter of an hour past teatime already. Miss Pepper will be all hot and bothered!"

They scrambled up. "If you come and whistle outside Rockingdown Cottage any time, we'll hear you and come out," said Roger. "I'll look out those plays for you."

"I'll see you tomorrow," said Barney, and stood watching them go, his blue eyes looking very far apart as he smiled and waved. Miranda waved a tiny paw too.

"I do like him," said Snubby. "Do you, Roger? And hasn't he got amazing eyes? Like somebody belonging to the Little Folk, not to us. That sounds silly – but you know what I mean."

They did know. There was something strange about Barney, something lonely and lost, and yet he was fun and had the most uproarious laugh, and the most natural manners in the world.

"I hope we see a lot of him," said Roger.

He needn't have worried about that – they were going to see far more of Barney than any of them guessed!

6

Mr King – and an Exciting Idea

The next thing that happened was that Miss Pepper found a tutor for the three of them. They were helping Mrs Round to clear away breakfast when he arrived. He knocked and rang, and Mrs Round scurried to open the door.

"Gentleman to see Miss Pepper," she announced to the children. "Name of King."

Diana hurried to fetch Miss Pepper, who took Mr King into the study and remained there with him for some time. Then she opened the door and called the three children. "Mr King, these are the three I told you about – they are cousins: this is Roger, this is Diana, this is Peter."

Roger and Diana looked surprised to hear Snubby called Peter. They had quite forgotten that that was really his name. Mr King grinned at them all. He was a stocky, well-built man about thirty-five or forty, with hair going a little grey, and a mouth that looked distinctly firm.

"They don't look too bad," he told Miss Pepper. She smiled.

"Appearances don't always tell the truth," she said. "Children, this is Mr King. Subject to final arrangements, he is going to come and give you the tutoring your parents want you to have."

This wasn't so good. The children's smiles faded away. They looked more carefully at Mr King. He looked back. Did they like him or didn't they? Snubby decided that he didn't. Diana wasn't sure. Roger felt that he might like him when he knew him better. Their hearts all sank when they thought of lessons morning after morning, just when they had got used to nice free days.

"Mr King will start with you on Monday next," said Miss Pepper.

"Can Loony be in the room too?" said Snubby.

Mr King looked a little startled. "Er – who is Loony?" he asked, wondering if there was another child, not quite so bright as these appeared.

"My spaniel," said Snubby, and at that moment Loony chose to make one of his usual hurricane-like appearances. He came in at the door like a rocket, and hurled himself at everyone as if he hadn't seen them for a year. He even rolled over Mr King's feet, too, before he realised that they were the feet of a stranger, and then he leaped to his own feet and growled.

"Oh, so this is Loony," said Mr King. "Well, I don't see why he shouldn't be in the room, if he doesn't disturb us."

Snubby immediately decided that he liked Mr King very much after all. Miss Pepper spoke hurriedly.

"I shouldn't make any rash promises if I were you," she said, trying to give Mr King a warning look. He saw it.

"Ah – yes – I won't promise," he said, and then as Loony tore at his shoe and got his shoelaces undone, he firmly added a few more words. "In fact, we'll put Loony on trial first."

"I wish Miranda could come too," said Snubby. "She's a monkey, Mr King – really a pet!"

Mr King thought it was time to go before he was asked to put a monkey on trial too.

He went, and Miss Pepper spoke to the three children.

"He has the most excellent references, and I think he should be a very fine tutor. You'll begin on Monday – and if I hear of you misbehaving, Snubby, I shall put Loony into a kennel at night instead of letting him sleep in the house."

This was a very alarming threat, and one that Miss Pepper was quite capable of carrying out. Snubby slept with Loony on his bed all night long, and the spaniel would be broken-hearted if he had to sleep anywhere else. Snubby didn't dare argue with Miss Pepper about this. He sneezed violently, and then sneezed twice more, fishing for his handkerchief with a most concerned expression. "Whoooosh-oo! Oh dear, I'm so sorry, Whhooooooooo . . ."

"Have you got a cold, Snubby?" said Miss Pepper. "I told you to take your jacket yesterday evening."

"No – no cold, Miss Pepper," said Snubby, finding an extremely dirty handkerchief and sneezing into that. "Just – whoooosh-oo – sorry, just a little pepper up my nose. Whoooooooo . . ."

Miss Pepper made an impatient noise and went out. Diana and Roger roared with laughter. Loony joined in the excitement and tore round the table six times without stopping.

"Racehorse trick being performed," said Snubby, putting away his hanky. "All right Loony – you've passed the winning-post about three times. Whoa!"

"What shall we do today?" asked Diana, as she finished clearing the breakfast table for Mrs Round.

"Let's go and peep in at the old mansion," said Roger. "Ask Mrs Round if there's any way of getting in. I'd just love to poke round it, and imagine what it was like in the old days."

Mrs Round didn't know very much. "You keep away from it," she said. "Folks do say that once a young fellow managed to get in there, and he couldn't never get out again. That might happen to you too. There's doors there that shut of themselves, yes, and lock themselves too. And there's rooms full of furniture, left by the last owner – my, they'll be full of moths and spiders! A strange, creepy place I wouldn't go into, not if you paid me a thousand pounds!"

This sounded pleasantly eerie. The three children at once made up their minds to do a bit of snooping that very day. They would meet Barney and take him too.

So when they heard Barney's soft whistle they went out to see him. He had Miranda on his shoulder. She leaped into a tree and peered into a window nearby. Mrs Round was in the room, sweeping. The monkey made a soft chattering noise.

Mrs Round looked up and was extremely surprised to see Miranda apparently about to jump in at the open window. She shut it at once, almost catching the monkey's nose. Then she stood at the window, shaking her fist at the surprised monkey. She called to Miss Pepper. "You come here, Miss Pepper, and see what those children have collected now!"

Miss Pepper hurried in, wondering what caterpillar or beetle or mouse Mrs Round had found. She was always finding something in Roger's bedroom. She was startled to see the monkey. Miranda disappeared down the tree.

"All I say is – if they starts bringing in monkeys I'm going," said Mrs Round. "Loony dogs I can put up with, beetles and such I can deal with, but monkeys, no. It'll be elephants next, trampling up the stairs and down."

Miss Pepper hurried downstairs to solve the monkey mystery. She saw Barney with the others; Miranda was on his shoulder. He nodded his head politely to her when the children introduced him. "Miss Pepper, this is Barnabas, and this is Miranda, his monkey. Isn't she sweet?"

Miss Pepper wasn't going to go so far as to say that. In her experience, monkeys were full of fleas and apt to bite people. She eyed Miranda mistrustfully.

"I'd rather you didn't bring that animal indoors," said Miss Pepper firmly. "Sweet or not, I'd rather she stayed outside."

"Yes, certainly, Miss Pepper," said Barney. "It isn't everyone that likes monkeys."

Miranda looked at Miss Pepper just as mournfully and pathetically as Loony sometimes looked at her. Oh dear, these animals! Why did they look at you like that? Miss Pepper ran to the kitchen, got a cucumber end and sliced it up. She ran out with the little slices on a plate. "Monkeys like cucumber," she said. "Here's some for her. But please take her down the garden. Oh, do be careful Loony doesn't chew her tail!"

Miranda's tail hung down and Loony was eyeing it hopefully. It did look nice and chewy. He made a snap at it and Miranda gave a leap off Barney's shoulder and sat on his head, chattering.

"Loony! If you dare to chew Miranda's tail I'll let her chew yours," said Snubby. Loony promptly sat down on his as if he understood every word. Barney gave one of his uproarious laughs and set everyone else laughing too. Even Mrs Round opened the bedroom window and looked out to see what the joke was.

"Come on," said Roger to Barney. "Let's go down the garden. Oh, wait a bit. I say, Miss Pepper, Barney's keen on reading Shakespeare's plays. He's read *The Tempest* and he wants me to lend him another. What would be a good one for him to read next?"

Miss Pepper was most surprised. What with his monkey, and his strange blue eyes, and now his liking for plays, this boy was puzzling. He looked quite a nice boy, and Miss Pepper wondered where he came from. She would have to ask Roger about him when he had gone.

"Well – he could try *A Midsummer Night's Dream*," she said.

"Oh yes, that's a lovely play," said Diana. "We did it once at school. I was Titania."

They went down the garden to a tumble-down summerhouse and sat there, with Loony on the floor trying to get another chew at Miranda's tail, and Miranda first on Snubby's shoulder and then Barney's – always swinging her tail just a little out of Loony's reach. She was very naughty. She took Diana's hanky out of her pocket and produced a horrible sticky mass of toffee from Snubby's shorts, which she proceeded to lick with great enjoyment before she threw the rest down to Loony.

"You're not to eat it, Loony," ordered Snubby. "You know what happened to you last time you ate toffee."

"What happened?" asked Barney, with interest.

"He got his top and bottom teeth stuck together," said Snubby. "And he was in such a fright that he rushed straight out-of-doors and down the street and didn't come back for hours, till the toffee had melted and gone. For a whole day after that he was scared. It's the only day I've ever known him be really good from morning to night."

"Miranda only licks it," said Barney.

"She's sensible," said Diana. "Loony isn't."

"Let's tell Barney what we want to do this morning," said Roger. "Barney, we want to go and walk round that big old mansion whose chimneys you can just see from here. It's empty now, nobody lives there, and there are all kinds of strange stories about it. We thought it would be fun to snoop round it."

They all got up, Loony too, his tail wagging. Were they going for a walk? He didn't like this sitting about. It was boring. They made their way through the overgrown paths, working their way steadily towards the old house.

"You almost have to hack your way through," said Roger. "We'll come to the drive soon – that's fairly clear. Look, now you can see the house. Enormous, isn't it?"

It certainly was. Great chimneys stood up from the roof, scores of windows peered out dimly, half-covered with ivy creeper, and there was an air of desolation and decay about the place.

"Come on," said Roger. "We'll explore, and I say, wouldn't it be fun if we managed to get inside!"

7

A Little Exploring

The four children and Loony came right up to the old house. A sparrow darted out of the thick ivy nearby and made them jump.

"It's so quiet. Even the wind seems to have deserted the old mansion," said Roger.

"I don't like it at all," said Diana. "It's a horrid place."

They came to the great flight of steps that led up to the front door. The stone steps were cracked in places and weeds sprouted through the cracks. One step wobbled when Roger stood on it. The foundations had rotted away.

"It would need an absolute fortune spent on it to make it liveable in," said Diana. "Still – I can quite well imagine how cheerful and lovely it must have been when it was properly looked after and a happy family lived in it."

They walked up to the great front door. It was a double one, and had a lot of iron-work about it which had rusted. There was no knocker, but a great iron bell-pull hung down beside the door.

Of course Snubby had to pull it. He found it very heavy and stiff to pull down and he almost hung on it to pull it. And suddenly a tremendous jangling broke out somewhere in the old house. It startled the children and Snubby let go of the bell-pull. Loony barked madly and scraped at the front door.

"Gosh – that made me jump," said Diana. "Who would have thought the bell rang after all these years! I guess it gave a fright to any rats and mice in the house. You are an idiot, Snubby. For goodness sake don't go ringing all the bells you see. You might break one."

"I don't see that that would matter," said Snubby. "I'm the only person ever likely to ring the bells here!"

There was no letterbox so the children could not peep through that. But there was a crack in the door and by putting their eye to it the children could see into the vast, dim hall.

It was not a pleasant sight. It was covered in grey dust, and the walls were festooned with cobwebs. It looked lost and forgotten and dead. A great staircase loomed up dimly in the distance, at the back of the hall.

Roger pushed the door hard, but he couldn't open it or budge it an inch, of course. Not that he really hoped to! Barney laughed at him.

"It would need a giant to force that door open!" he said. "Come on – let's look in through the windows. There are plenty of them!"

They went down the flight of stone steps and made their way round the east side of the house. They came to some large french windows. The glass was dirty and streaked but they were able to see in. It must once have been a ballroom, with a beautiful floor. Built-in mirrors still had their places on the walls. Most of them were now cracked. The children saw their ghostly faces reflected in the mirror opposite the window through which they were peeping. It made them jump.

"I really thought it was somebody looking at us," said Diana, scared, "but it's only our reflections in that cracked mirror. What a lovely room this must have been! What are those broken things in that corner?"

Roger squinted at them. "Broken chairs, I think," he said. "You know we heard this place was used in the last war for something or other. I expect this was one of the rooms used. Those look like office chairs or something."

They went on round the house, peeping into window after window, peering into dim, dusty rooms that had a look of utter forlornness. It made the children feel quite depressed. Even Miranda and Loony were quiet and subdued.

They came right round the house, back to the front door again. Not one window had been found unfastened, nor even cracked or broken. One or two had shutters fastened across them and these windows might have been broken. The children couldn't see.

They looked at the upstairs windows. They seemed tight-shut too, and again some had shutters fastened across them.

"Look!" said Diana, pointing. "There are two windows there with bars across. That must have been the children's nursery. When Roger and I were small we had bars like that across our windows too. We used to hate them."

Snubby was squinting up at the windows, blinking in his efforts to focus them clearly, for they were rather high up. "You know, it almost looks to me as if there are curtains at those windows," he said. "Can any of you see?"

Barney had the best eyesight of them all. His bright blue eyes fastened on the nursery windows. "Yes!" he said in surprise. "There are curtains there, almost falling to bits, I think!"

They all stared up at the barred nursery windows, Loony too. Miranda suddenly left Barney's shoulder, leaped up the ivy, bounded on to a windowsill, flung herself upwards again to a little balcony, and then there she was, sitting on the windowsill of the old nursery window, peering in!

"I wish I could do that!" said Snubby in admiration.

"I'm surprised you can't!" said Roger.

They were all watching Miranda. She sat on the windowsill, and then she suddenly got between the bars and disappeared! Everyone gasped.

"Where's she gone?" said Diana, amazed.

"Into the room behind!" said Barney.

"But isn't there any glass there?" said Roger.

"Apparently not," said Diana. "Or she wouldn't have been able to go in! How peculiar!"

"Wait a bit," said Barney, squinting up at the window. "I think I can see where it's broken – just at one side, look. There's a hole there as if a stone's been thrown through or something. That's where Miranda went through."

She appeared again and looked down at the very interested children. She chattered and waved her tiny paw. "She's found something interesting up there," said Barney at once. "There – she's gone into the room again. Whatever can she have found?"

Miranda appeared once more and this time she was holding something. She held it out and they all tried to see what it was.

"Throw it down, Miranda!" shouted Barney. And down through the air came the thing Miranda was holding. It fell beside Diana's foot. Loony pounced on it at once and Diana had to wrench it from him. She held it out to the others.

"A doll! A funny old-fashioned rag-doll! Would you believe it! Fancy Miranda finding it in the old nursery!"

"She loves dolls," said Barney, and he took it and examined it. He shook it and dust flew from it in a cloud. He looked at it thoughtfully. "I wonder if there's anything else there?" he said. And as if Miranda could read his thoughts she appeared again at the window with something else in her paws. She held it out, chattering – then down it came, turning over and over in the air. Barney caught it. He gave an exclamation and showed it to the others.

"A soldier on horseback – carved most beautifully!" said Roger, taking it. "Look at it. The colour's still showing. What lovely soldiers children must have had in the old days – I never had ones like this."

"Must be part of a hand-made set," said Diana. They all looked at the beautiful model and then gazed upwards again. And Miranda threw down yet another thing!

This time it was a book. It fell to pieces as Miranda threw it and the pages fluttered

in the air. Diana picked some of them up.
"What a funny old book!" she said. "It's
rather like one Granny has, on her special
bookshelf – she keeps a collection of children's books that are very precious because
they are more than a hundred years old. I
say, it's strange, isn't it, that there are still
curtains to that room and toys there. What
do you make of it, Roger?"

"I don't know," said Roger. "Except that perhaps when the house was let, the nursery was locked up because of memories or something; you known how grown-ups sometimes feel about those things. Think how Mummy keeps the first dress you ever wore, Di, and the first tooth of mine that came out. She just won't part with them."

"Mothers seem to be like that," said Diana. "Perhaps the mother of the children who had these toys couldn't bear to let strangers use her nursery – couldn't bear to part with the toys and things – and locked them up. Perhaps the rooms were forgotten. It's such a big house they might quite well have been."

Miranda appeared again. Barney called up to her. "No, Miranda. No more."

But one more thing came floating down, spreading itself out in the air. It was a small handkerchief. Diana caught it as it floated by her head. In the corner, beautifully embroidered, was a name in what once had been pale blue silk: Bob. Just that and nothing more. The children looked at the name. Who was Bob? Was he grown-up now or was he dead long ago? They didn't know. They pictured a tiny boy being told to use his hanky – the one with his name on. Diana could almost hear his nurse speaking to him:

"Don't sniff, Bob, dear. Use your hanky –

the one with your name on. I gave it to you this morning."

"Come down, Miranda!" called Barney. He turned to the others. "She'll throw down everything in the room if I don't stop her," he said. "And goodness knows how much more is still up there. I wouldn't be surprised if the nursery is still furnished, with cots and things. Odd, isn't it?"

Miranda came leaping down. It was astonishing how she could come safely down the walls, just by clutching lightly at the ivy here and there.

Loony greeted her with a mad series of barks. He was jealous because she could do so many things that he couldn't. She settled on Barney's shoulder, and took hold of his right ear with her tiny paw. She made a funny whispering sound in his ear. He shook his head like a dog.

"Don't! You tickle!"

"What are we going to do with these things?" said Diana. "They don't belong to us."

"Well, we can't possibly put them back," said Snubby. "Unless we tell Miranda to – and surely she wouldn't have the sense to take them all back."

"Oh, yes, she would," said Barney. "She'll do anything I tell her. You don't know how clever she is. I should think she's just about the cleverest monkey in the world. If people knew how clever she was they'd offer me a thousand pounds for her – and I wouldn't take it."

They all gazed at Miranda with respect. A thousand pounds! "Why that's more than I'm worth!" said Snubby.

"I should think so! About nine hundred and ninety-nine pounds, ninety-nine pence more," said Roger at once. "Work that out, Snubby."

Snubby couldn't. He changed the subject and looked longingly up at the barred windows. "I wish we could get up there!" he said.

"Well," said Barney, surprisingly. "That's easy – if you really want to."

8

Barney Has an Idea

"What do you mean?" said Roger, staring at Barney in surprise. "We can't possibly get up there – why, it's three storeys up, and pretty high storeys at that. No ladder we've got would reach there even if we'd got one, which we haven't."

"And it would be too heavy to carry if we had," said Diana, remembering how heavy the longest ladder at home had been when she had tried to carry it with Roger.

"I'm not thinking of a ladder," said Barney. "I'm thinking of a rope."

They all stared at him. "A rope?" repeated Roger. "But how in the world are you going to get a rope up there. You'd want a ladder to take up the rope!"

Barney laughed one of his loud laughs. "No, no, I'd just send Miranda up with a rope. She'll do anything like that."

Still they didn't understand. Barney grinned at them.

"It's plain you've never lived in a circus

or a fair," he said. "You get used to puzzles of this sort there. Now look – if we get a rope, we give one end to Miranda and up she goes to the nursery windows with it. She sits on the windowsill and twists the rope over the bars, then she throws the rope down to us. It comes slithering down the walls and down to us. We catch it – and we've got a double rope then, haven't we, with the middle held by those bars up there! And it's easy enough to test the bars by pulling on the rope."

"And then up we go to the windowsill!" cried Roger, seeing light. "Gosh – that's an idea. All the same, I don't think I could climb a rope all that way. I'm pretty good at gym, and one of the best on the ropes at school, but it's a terrific way up to those windows."

"I shall be able to manage all right," said Barney. "I've been on the ropes at the circus many a time – on the tightrope too. You should see me walk along it backwards!"

The others looked at Barney with a new respect. Could he really walk on a rope or a wire? Snubby made up his mind to get him to teach him during the holidays. He imagined himself setting up a rope across the gym and walking airily along it. That would make the others stare!

"Climbing up a rope's nothing," said Barney. "It's a question whether those bars will still hold. Now the thing is, where is there a rope? I haven't got one – have you?"

Roger didn't know. His exploration of Rockingdown Cottage hadn't shown him any ropes or ladders.

"Even if there isn't a rope at the cottage we can buy one," he said. "I say – this is exciting, isn't it? Do you think you really could get into that window, Barney?"

"Sure of it," said Barney. "Miranda can easily take up the rope. She knows how to put it over the bars – she's done that often enough in the circus. Then I'll go up and see what I can see. If there's a hole big enough for Miranda to get through, it will be big enough for me to put my hand in to slip the catch of the window, and in I'll go!"

"Let's go and buy the rope at once," Diana said eagerly.

With Loony rushing ahead like a mad thing, the four of them made their way back through the grounds. They went down the overgrown drive, as that was the shortest way to the village. They had decided that it wouldn't be much use looking for a rope at Rockingdown Cottage. Miss Pepper would be sure to ask what they were looking for and why they wanted a rope and a hundred other things.

"Grown-ups are terribly inquisitive," said

Snubby, plaintively. "Even if I'm doing absolutely nothing at all people come and ask me what I'm up to."

"I don't blame them," said Diana. "You're always up to some kind of mischief as far as I can see. By the way, was it you who put my bedroom slippers on the top of the cupboard last night? I couldn't find them for ages."

"I expect I put them there out of Loony's way," said Snubby.

"Well, don't. Just shut my bedroom door if it happens to be open, then Loony can't go in," said Diana. "I'm not going to hunt all over the place for my slippers every single night!"

They decided to have an ice cream at the little general store when they got there. They went inside and ordered vanilla ices. The old lady got them out of the freezer.

"And how do you like Rockingdown Cottage?" she said. "Nice little place, isn't it? No strange stories about it, like there are about the big house."

"What strange stories are there?" said Roger, paying for the ice creams.

"Oh, I wouldn't scare you with such tales," said the old woman, beaming. "That old place has fallen on evil days. Seems as if a curse was on it, somehow, the things that have happened." This sounded interesting.

"What happened?" asked Roger.

"Oh, folks were killed and two children died, and . . ."

"What two children?" asked Diana. "Was one of them called Bob?"

"Well, there now – fancy you knowing that!" said the old woman in surprise. "Yes, that was Master Robert. His sister, little Arabella, fell out of the nursery window and was killed – then only Master Robert was left. So they barred the windows up. And then if he didn't go and get scarlet fever and pass away too."

"What happened then?" asked Diana, after a pause. Poor little Bob! She actually had his small hanky in her pocket. He hadn't lived to grow up but his hanky was still there. And his soldier and book.

"The nursery was shut up just as it was," said the old woman, trying to remember. "The nurse was given order to leave everything as it was – everything! She was so upset, poor creature, she loved those two children like her own."

"What happened to the father and mother?" asked Roger.

"Lord Rockingdown was killed," said the old woman. "Yes, and his lady died of a broken heart – no husband, no child left. Wasn't I telling you this the other day? I'll be boring you, repeating myself like this! The estate went to a cousin after that, but he never came near it."

The children now had a picture of what happened to the unlucky house and family. Diana felt sad. She imagined the big house happy and lively, with Lord and Lady Rockingdown giving parties, going off to hunt, choosing ponies for their two small children, Arabella and Robert – planning all sorts of things for them as they grew up.

But they didn't grow up. The time came when the happy family was no more; the house was empty and unloved. Only the nursery with their toys, and goodness knew what else, were left to guard the memories of the little family.

Diana's eyes had been wandering round the crowded little shop. It really was a most interesting place and Diana felt that there was practically nothing that couldn't be bought there. Pails, deckchairs, lengths of garden hose, saucepans, kettles, rugs, crockery – everything seemed to be there, muddled up together. Things hung down from the ceiling, and were piled on the shelves round the walls.

"Do you know exactly what you've got in your shop?" Diana asked curiously. "There are so many things – surely you don't know them all."

"Ah, indeed I do," said the old woman, a smile on her wrinkled pink face. "There's not a thing I don't know, and I could put my hand on anything you like to mention!"

"Well, could you put your hand on a good, long, strong rope?" said Roger at once.

"A rope? Now, let's see," said the old woman, frowning. "Yes, second shelf to the right, near the end. That's where it should be."

"I'll look for you," said Barney. "Don't you go climbing about on those shelves!"

The second shelf was near the ceiling. Barney leaped up like a cat, found the rope, and leaped back again.

"What it is to be young!" said the old woman admiringly. "You ought to be in a circus, you ought!"

Everyone grinned, but nobody said anything. The old woman looked at the price on the rope. "Do you really want a rope?" she said. "Don't you go doing nothing dangerous now. This rope's expensive, but then it's good and strong. Perhaps a cheaper one would do for you. What do you want it for?"

"Oh, this and that," said Diana quickly. "I think a strong one would be best. Pay for it, Roger."

Roger paid, thinking it was a good thing it was the beginning of the holidays and he had plenty of money!

They said goodbye and went off with the rope. As they went down the street the church clock struck loudly.

"Half past twelve already," said Diana. "We shan't have time to do any more exploring this morning. We'd better meet you this afternoon, Barney."

"Right," said Barney.

"What are you going to do about lunch?" asked Snubby, suddenly realising that Barney had no nice-smelling meal to go home to – in fact, not even a home.

"I'll buy myself some bread and cheese," said Barney. "And I'll get Miranda an orange. She loves oranges."

He went off with Miranda on his shoulder, after arranging to call for the children at half past two. Diana made up her mind to ask Miss Pepper to give them a picnic tea – one they could share with Barney.

She was worried about Barney. Was it comfortable to sleep under a hedge at night? Did he have enough money to buy himself the food he wanted? Suppose it rained? What did he do then? He didn't seem to have any clothes except those he had on. What a strange life he must lead with Miranda – just the two of them, wandering about together. She looked up.

"It's going to pour," she said to the others. "I hope Miss Pepper won't say we're to keep indoors this afternoon."

"It'll hold off until the evening," said Roger, looking at the clouds. "We'll be all right this afternoon, I think. There may be a storm tonight."

Miss Pepper was pleased to see them punctual for once. An appetising smell filled the house as they went in.

"Sausages and onions," said Roger. "I hope there are chips."

There were – and fried tomatoes too. The children were hungry and soon cleared the big dish. Diana wished Barney could have shared such a meal. She pictured him sitting on a grassy bank somewhere, munching bread and cheese, with Miranda beside him, eating an orange.

"Never mind, he'll be with us this afternoon, sharing our tea – and a splendid adventure!" she thought.

9

Barney Climbs the Rope

Barney was outside at half past two, whistling. "There's that boy with the monkey again," said Miss Pepper. "I do hope he's a nice boy, Roger. I don't want you to make friends with anyone who will lead you into bad ways."

Roger grinned. "It's much more likely that Snubby will teach him bad ways," he said. "Barney's all right, Miss Pepper. Shall I ask him in for a meal sometime, then you can judge for yourself?"

"Yes. That would be a good idea," said Miss Pepper. "Well, you'd better go, if he's waiting for you. I've got your picnic ready for you. It's on the kitchen windowsill. Ask Mrs Round for it."

Snubby went racing round to the kitchen, Loony at his heels. "Roundy, Roundy, where are you? Have you got our tea for us?"

Mrs Round looked up from her cup of tea. "Now don't you be cheeky," she said. "Calling me Roundy like that. I've told you about that before, Master Sauce-Box!"

"Roundy's a lovely name for you," said Snubby, and gave the plump Mrs Round a sudden squeeze. "I can't help calling you Roundy. It's a pet name. You needn't mind."

Mrs Round didn't. She thought Snubby was what she called a "caution", and she didn't seem to mind what he said or did. She was even putting up with Loony a bit better now, in spite of his habit of taking all her brushes out into the garden.

"That dog and you are a pair," she said, putting her hair straight after Snubby's sudden squeeze. "Get down, Loony. Where did you put my carpet brush, I'd like to know? Wait till I find it and I'll give you such a hiding with it."

Loony picked up a duster and ran off with it, shaking it as if it were a rat. Snubby yelled at him and Miss Pepper appeared in the doorway.

"Snubby! Stop that noise. What's the dog got now? Drop it, Loony! I'm so sorry, Mrs Round – that dog is completely mad."

"That's all right, Miss Pepper," Mrs Round said graciously. "I'm getting used to him now. He's not so bad, taken all round. Just puppy-like."

Miss Pepper was relieved to hear Mrs Round taking things so calmly. She gave Snubby the basket of tea things and sent him off. He tore into the garden with

Loony, who greeted Barney riotously. Miranda sat on her master's shoulder and watched. She suddenly slid down and caught hold of Loony's ear. She gave it a good tug and leaped back again to Barney's shoulder almost before the dog knew what had happened. He yelped.

The children laughed. They enjoyed these bits of by-play between Loony and Miranda. "We've got the tea," said Diana. "And the rope. Come on!"

Feeling rather excited the children made their way once more through the grounds to the old mansion. Miranda made a little chattering noise when they came near. She remembered her adventure of the morning.

"Oh no! It's beginning to rain!" said Roger. "Just as we've got a picnic tea too!"

"We can have it on that veranda place," said Snubby, pointing to where a veranda showed on the south side of the house, almost hidden by hanging creepers. "We could drag away some of those creepers to let a bit of light and air in."

They put the tea basket on the veranda. It was certainly a dismal place. Diana felt sure it would be full of spiders and earwigs, and very damp. She hoped they wouldn't have to have tea there.

The boys were longing to get on with the exploring. They were already walking round to the part of the house where the nursery was. They looked up at the barred windows. Miranda was off Barney's shoulder and away to the nursery windowsill immediately. Barney called her back.

"Here, Miranda! Come back. We've got a job for you to do!"

Snubby and Roger undid the rope. It certainly was a good strong one. "I believe it will be too heavy for Miranda to pull up behind her," said Roger weighing it in his hand. It certainly was very heavy.

"I thought of that," said Barney, and he took some string from his pocket. "We'll play the old trick of letting a string pull the rope!"

The others watched while he tied some string to the rope-end. Then he found a stone with a hole in it and tied the other end of string to it.

"What's that for?" said Diana.

"You'll soon see," said Barney. "Now, Miranda – are you ready? Take the string up – twist it over the bars just as you do when you go up to one of the trapeze swings in the circus – and let the other end of the string drop!"

Miranda listened, her brown eyes gleaming intelligently. She chattered softly back. She really was a remarkable little monkey.

She took the stone in her tiny paw and leaped off Barney's shoulder. She bounded to the little balcony, pulling the string up behind her. Up the ivy, then on to another windowsill and up the ivy again to the barred windows. The string unravelled swiftly behind her.

Miranda sat on the windowsill, peering in at the window again. Barney called to her, "Go on, Miranda. Do your stuff!"

The others watched breathlessly. Would Miranda really "do her stuff"?

She did! She slipped the stone over the top bar, and let it drop down the other side of the bars – the window side. The stone fell, dragging the string behind it. More string unravelled and ran up the wall, as the stone with its tail of string dropped down to the ground.

Barney caught the stone as it fell and pulled the string. "Now watch," he said to Diana. "You'll soon see the rope go up."

He pulled hard at the string, and it travelled over the bars of the window and down the wall to his hand – dragging behind it the rope that was tied to it. Up went the rope after the string, round the bars, and down to Barney's hand, as he pulled.

"It's very, very clever," said Diana, much impressed. "Barney, I should never have thought of that."

"Oh, there's nothing at all in that," said Barney, smiling. "Any circus kid could do that from the age of two. Hello – Miranda's gone into the room again. I'd better go up

before she starts showering us with all kinds of things!"

He twisted the rope as the two strands hung from the bars to the ground. He twisted it so thoroughly that the two strands looked like one. They would be very strong, and give him a good hold.

"Now, let's hope those bars will hold all right," said Barney. He put all his weight suddenly on the rope and pulled hard. There was an ominous grating noise.

"Oh – the top bar's giving way," said Diana in alarm. "Look out – it may fall!"

Barney put his weight on the rope again. The top bar came out of the wall at one side and hung down crookedly. The rope slid down to the next bar. There were five bars all together.

"Well – that's one bar gone," said Barney. "Perhaps the next one will hold." Again he put all his weight on the rope. The second bar gave a very little bit, and then held.

"I'll try going up now," said Barney. "Don't worry if this bar breaks. The rope will just slide down to the next one – and if that one breaks it will go down to the fourth one."

"Yes, but, Barney, suppose they all break?" said Diana in a panic.

"By the time that happens I'll be on the windowsill," said Barney, with a grin. "Don't worry. I'm like a cat, I always fall on my feet."

He suddenly swung on the rope, slid up his legs, holding the rope between his feet, and then hauled himself up strongly. "He's going up!" said Snubby, and Loony leaped at the rope in excitement, barking.

"The bar's breaking!" screamed Diana. "Look out, Barney – it's breaking!"

Sure enough, it suddenly gave way and dropped out from the wall, striking the stone sill as it fell, and just missing hitting Loony on the head. He jumped away in fright and went to hide under a bush.

Barney felt the rope drop a little and got a jerk as it came to rest on the next bar. He hung still for a moment. What about this bar?

That held for a few seconds only, and then it too broke from its place. It didn't fall but hung down to one side and the rope slid down to the fourth bar.

"Barney, come down! All the bars will break and you'll hurt yourself!" shrieked Diana, really frightened. Barney took no notice. He went on hauling himself up the rope, intent on reaching the windowsill before the last bar broke. Once the fourth one broke, there was only one bar left.

The fourth one broke just as he reached the windowsill. With a light, catlike motion he was over the last bar and on to the broad sill. He sat there, grinning down at the others, the rope swinging below him. Diana was pale with fright.

"Well, I'm here!" called Barney, getting his breath back after his long climb. He glanced into the window behind him to look for Miranda. He looked into the room there for what seemed a long, long time to the children below.

"Barney! What can you see?" called Snubby impatiently, longing to see everything himself.

"It's weird!" called down Barney at last. "The room in here is a proper nursery, rocking-horse and all, and there's even a meal laid on the table. Gives me a funny feeling!"

Diana shivered a little. It certainly did sound strange. "Can we come up the rope too?" she called. "Can you tie it to something in the room?"

"You're none of you coming up the rope," said Barney. "You can't climb like me. You'd kill yourselves."

He put his arm in at the hole in the glass of the window – the hole Miranda used when she went in and out. He felt about for the window-catch. Would it be too old and rusty to move? He didn't want to have to break the window much more.

He found the catch. It certainly was stiff – but he moved it at last. Then the window stuck, of course! It took a lot of shoving and pushing to make it move a little way. Barney almost fell off the windowsill in his efforts to open it. But at last it was open far enough for him to squeeze in. He disappeared, while the children below watched eagerly and impatiently.

Barney looked round the room. It had a carpet on the floor, almost eaten away by moths. The window curtains were also in holes, destroyed by moths. A nursery table, covered by what had once been a pretty patterned cloth, stood in the middle of the room. Coloured nursery chairs stood about.

A big rocking-horse stood near the window. Barney touched it with his foot. It rocked, creaking to and fro. It sent a cold shiver down his back.

A big doll's-house stood on the low shelf. A box of bricks was upset on the floor nearby. Books stood on a bookshelf, mostly picture books – Bob and Arabella apparently had not been very old. Dead embers of a coal fire still showed.

"It must have been shut up and left very suddenly," thought Barney. "Nothing tidied up, nothing cleared away, just left exactly as it was when Bob was taken ill."

He saw another door leading out of the nursery and went to it. It was half open. There was another room beyond. In this room were two small beds – evidently one for each child. A low dressing-table and two little chests-of-drawers stood near the window. Yet another door opened out from this middle room to what must have been the nurse's room. It was neat and tidy, covered with dust, and not so much eaten up by clothes moths. The bed stood in the corner with its once-white cover now grey with dust. It was all very strange indeed. Barney felt as if he had stepped back years and years.

A voice came up from below. "Barney! Barney! What are you doing? You might come and tell us what's up there!"

10

In the Old Forgotten House

Barney went back to the window through which he had climbed. He leaned out.

"It's all very peculiar," he said. "There are three rooms up here – still furnished. Wait, I'll come down and tell you all about it. Somehow I don't feel as if I want to shout."

"Barney! There's only one bar left!" shouted Diana in a panic. "Don't risk that. Tie the rope to something else in the room."

Barney tried the last bar with his hand. It broke at once. It was the rottenest one of all. Thank goodness he hadn't had to trust his weight to that one. Then he looked at the rope. It was almost in two! It had pulled against something jagged on one of the bars and was cut practically to the last thread. Even as he took it up it fell in half. He made a grab at it – but down it went.

There was a dismayed silence. "Now what's going to happen?" asked Diana. "The rope's in two!"

"We can knot it, silly," said Roger.

Barney leaned out of the window and pointed up to the sky.

"Look there – there's a rainstorm just about to pour down. You'll all get soaked if you mess about knotting the rope and sending Miranda up with it. I think I'd better see if I can get out of this room and into the main part of the building. Then I can open a door or something from inside and let you in."

"Right," said Roger. "We'll go and wait on that veranda, Barney. It's beginning to pour now."

Roger, Snubby, Diana and Loony ran round the house to the horrible veranda. As Diana had feared, there were spiders and earwigs, and many other insects she felt she had never seen anywhere else. The floor was slimy and the place felt very damp. It was quite impossible to think of having tea there.

"I hope Barney will find some way of letting us in," said Snubby with a shiver. "It's jolly cold now."

He sneezed.

"Pepper up your nose," said Roger, trying to raise a laugh. But the veranda was too gloomy a place for a joke or a laugh.

What was Barney doing in the old house? Was he finding a way to let them in? He was certainly doing his best. He went to the outer door of the nursery. It was not locked.

In fact, the key was in the keyhole inside the room. He opened the door and looked out on a long dark passage. Surely these rooms had been locked – not left open for anyone to come into?

He went down the passage, disturbing the dust on the floor. It rose in a light cloud. One or two long cobwebby strands hanging from the ceiling brushed against his face and made him jump. They felt like soft fingers. He didn't like it at all, and wished he had a torch with him. The passage was so very dark.

He came to a stout door at the end of the passage. He tried it, turning the big handle this way and that. No use. The door wouldn't open. It was well and truly locked on the other side. Of course, that was how they had sealed off the nursery – by locking the door that led to all three rooms. Nobody could go near them.

How could he get into the main part of the house? He considered the matter carefully. He could not possibly kick this stout door down, and the lock was strong. It looked as if he couldn't leave this passage at all.

A thought struck him. What about the key he had seen in one of the nursery doors? Would that by any chance fit this door? It was worth trying.

He went back quickly, almost choking as

he kicked up the dust. Miranda clung to his shoulder in silence. She didn't like this. It was strange and dark. She held on tightly to Barney's shoulder.

He looked at the three doors in the other rooms. Each had a key in it. He looked at the keys. They seemed more or less the same to him, but perhaps they weren't. He took them back to the passage door.

The first key slid in easily, but wouldn't turn. However he tried, it wouldn't turn more than halfway. He was afraid of forcing it in case the key broke in the lock. He tried the second one. That would only turn halfway too. Without much hope he tried the third key.

And it turned! True, it was stiff, and grated protestingly as he turned it slowly and carefully but it suddenly clicked back the old lock. He could open the door!

He turned the handle and pulled at the door. It came open and a cloud of dust arose again, making him cough. He was looking out at a broad landing. Doors opened on either side of it. Barney went to them, walking on tiptoe, he didn't quite know why.

He pushed open the doors, one by one, and looked into the rooms. They were completely empty. Not a chair, not a book, not a rug, remained in any of them. Only dust covered the bare floors, and cobwebs hung everywhere. Large spiders scuttled over the ceilings as he opened the doors, terrified to be disturbed in the midst of their long, dark peace.

Most of the rooms were dark, or at least dim, because of the ivy that grew across the windows, allowing only a small amount of daylight in. The rooms smelled musty and old.

Barney went down the bare stairs. Dust rose from each stair, fine dust like grey flour that made him choke whenever it reached his nose. He didn't touch the banister rail as he went down, for fear of disturbing even more dust.

Down to the first floor. Here there were more doors that opened on to miserable dark rooms, dusty and silent. From the first floor down to the ground floor the staircase descended from each side of the great landing, and then joined its two flights together to sweep down in one huge curve to the enormous hall.

Now Barney was in the hall, which he had seen through the crack in the front door. He tiptoed to a big room to the right. It was the ballroom. The mirrors gave back a dozen reflections of his dim, shadowy figure and made him feel uncomfortable. He left the ballroom, for here, again, there was broken furniture, old papers strewn about and the remains of a broken telephone. It was dusty, but the dust was not so thick as in the upper rooms.

He went into another room, and saw that it was the room leading out on the veranda. He made out the figures of the three children, and Loony, standing patiently outside, waiting for him. Perhaps he could open the veranda door. He went over to it and knocked on the glass with his knuckles. All three children jumped violently and then turned to see what the noise was.

"It's Barney!" cried Diana gladly. "Oh, Barney – you were able to get out of the rooms upstairs, then!"

Barney could just make out what she said. He struggled with the veranda door-bolts and managed at last to push each one back. He unlocked the door and forced it open. The children outside rushed in, and Diana caught hold of his arm.

"Barney! You are clever! We were getting so cold out there, and the rain comes sweeping in on the veranda."

Loony tore round and round the room, kicking up dust as he went. "Stop that, Loony," said Roger sharply. "You'll choke us all – and yourself too."

Miranda still clung to Barney's shoulder. She was very glad to see the other children. They all looked round at the silent, dusty room. Diana took a few steps forward and then screamed, making the others jump.

She had walked into a cobweb, which had swung softly against her face. "Someone touched me," she yelled.

"No. It's only a hanging cobweb," said Barney with a laugh. "There are plenty of those. Has anyone got a torch?"

Snubby had. He usually had everything. It was really amazing what his pockets could hold. He fished out a torch and switched it on. Immediately a horde of spiders went this way and that and Diana screamed again. She couldn't bear spiders. The children saw the big webs everywhere and the long strands of web hanging down from the ceiling.

"I don't like this much," said Roger. "It's an awful place to have our tea in. What's the place upstairs like, Barney? You haven't told us anything yet."

Barney told them quickly what he had found, and how he had got out of the rooms and downstairs. "I think we'd be better up in the nursery really," he said. "It's frightfully dusty too, but at least there are chairs up there to sit on – and it seems lighter up there. Let's go up."

So they all went up, climbing first the two-branched stairway to the first floor and then the smaller one to the second floor. They came to the passage door and went through it.

"This must have been the nursery wing,

all on its own," said Barney. "A very nice place it was too, with a wonderful view over the countryside. Look!"

He swung open the nursery door and the children peered in. They fell silent when they saw the rocking-horse standing motionless as if waiting for some child to ride it, the toy-cupboard door open to show the toys still sitting there, the doll's-house on the shelf – and the plates and dishes on the table, set out ready for a meal.

"Weird," said Diana. "Weird to look at and weird to feel. I'm not sure I like it. Still, the house feels a bit happier here than it did downstairs."

"We'll have tea here," said Roger. "That's if nobody minds sitting down in all this dust! Come on! Where's the basket? I'll feel a lot better when I've got a few slices of cake inside me."

11

A Very Good Idea

The storm came while they sat eating their tea. Thunder suddenly rolled over the sky and lightning forked across, dazzling the children for a moment and making them jump and blink.

"Well, I'm glad we're not out-of-doors picnicking!" said Roger, trying to be cheerful. But nobody felt terribly happy. Still, they felt a lot better when they had eaten every sandwich, every cake and biscuit, and drunk some lemonade too. Loony had his share. Actually he was a real nuisance in that dusty room, because his four feet scraped the dust up so much. Miranda stayed sedately on her master's shoulder, nibbling small pieces of cucumber sandwich.

The children explored the three rooms again after tea. It seemed sad to think that they had never been used since little Bob had been taken away with scarlet fever so many, many years ago. "I suppose his mother couldn't bear to come into the empty rooms again," said Diana. "Poor thing! She couldn't even bear to have them touched. I wonder if anyone knows about them but us. They might quite easily have been forgotten by now. I mean, people might have thought that door in the passage outside that was locked was only the door to a boxroom or something."

"I think you're probably right," said Barney. "My word, hark at the rain pelting down!"

It certainly was pouring hard. The thunder still rolled across the sky, but sounded further away, and the lightning flashed but not so vividly. Diana glanced at Barney. Where would he sleep that night? Surely not under a hedge.

"Barney, you won't sleep out in the open tonight, surely?" she asked him at last, putting away the lemonade bottles in the empty basket. "Everywhere will be so wet."

"No, I shan't," said Barney. "As a matter of fact, I had thought about sleeping here."

The others looked at him in amazement.

"What, here! By yourself! In this awful old empty house, with its spiders and dust!" cried Diana horrified. "How could you dare to? All alone too!"

"I shall have Miranda," said Barney. "And I'm not easily scared, you know. I've slept in much worse places."

Diana couldn't think of any worse place

to sleep. She shuddered. Miranda put her little arms round Barney's neck and chattered to him.

"She says it's all right, she'll be with me and chase any spiders away," said Barney with a grin.

"I think it's a good idea," said Snubby. "After all, the beds are still good, even if the bedclothes fall to bits! The nurse's room didn't look too bad. Why don't you take that for your room, Barney? You'd be quite comfortable there."

"I know!" cried Diana, getting up and looking in various cupboards. "I'll see if there's a dustpan and brush somewhere – and I could perhaps clear up some of the dust in the nurse's room."

It was Loony who found the brush, of course! He darted into the bottom of a cupboard and brought out a carpet brush, whose bristles had gone soft. "Just the thing!" said Diana, wrenching the brush away from Loony. "Thanks, Loony. I'll have it. Snubby, keep him away from me – he's kicking up dust all over the place."

So while the boys amused themselves by looking through the old toy-cupboard and picking out more of the beautifully carved old soldiers, and Miranda tried on various dolls' bonnets, Diana got very busy.

She took the bedclothes off the nurse's bed and carried them down the passage to the landing. She shook them well. They were full of dust, of course. The bedspread and one of the blankets fell to pieces and were no use, but one blanket seemed quite good. Diana carried it back to the bed and laid it on the mattress. There were no sheets. Perhaps those had been removed by the nurse. The pillow was full of moths. They flew out as she punched it. Grubs had eaten the pillow almost to nothing.

"Barney will have to do without a pillow," she thought. "We must bring him an old coat or something, to roll up under his head. Or perhaps an old cushion."

She swept the dust off the dressing-table, the washstand and the chest of drawers. It choked her and she began to cough. She had to wait for the dust to settle a little before she went on. She went to the window and struggled to open it. The room was so musty and dusty, a little fresh air would be good. She got the window open at last and a shower of raindrops came over her as she pushed back the thick sprays of ivy.

That gave her an idea. She picked some of the rain-wet sprays and sprinkled the dusty floor with the raindrops. "That will help to lay the dust a bit," she thought, rather pleased with herself. It certainly did. She was able to sweep the floor carefully without raising too much dust now.

In the end she took up the moth-eaten

carpet and stuffed it into a cupboard. It fell to pieces as she brushed it. It was easier to brush the bare boards beneath.

She called Barney when she had finished. "It's the best I can do," she said. "It's not nearly so dusty now and you've got one fairly decent blanket to sleep on – or under. I don't know what you'll do for water, though."

"There's probably an old well somewhere, or a pump in the kitchen," said Barney cheerfully. Things like that didn't worry him at all. "Anyway, I always swim in the river each morning."

"There's a bottle of lemonade left," said Roger. "We'll leave you that. Well, I hope you'll be all right, Barney, sleeping here all by yourself!"

"It's fine," said Barney. "Better than a wet barn or a dripping hedge any day!"

"Will you leave the veranda door unlocked and unbolted?" said Roger. "Then we can get in and out as we like. So long as the door is shut no one will guess anything. We could use these rooms up here as play-rooms in wet weather."

"I'm glad Barney's got somewhere sheltered to sleep," said Diana. "And Miranda too, of course. Where is she?"

They went back to look for her. She had watched Barney stretching himself on the bed and had considered him carefully and then bounded out of the room. Now she had disappeared!

It was Loony who smelled her out. He rushed over to the wall opposite the window in the day nursery and barked madly. There was a doll's bed there, with a doll in it.

Beside the doll lay Miranda, her big brown eyes looking wickedly up at Loony. She was in bed too! If Barney had a bed, she would have one as well!

"Oh, Miranda!" cried Diana. "You look a darling there. Barney, isn't she sweet? Don't, Loony. You've pulled the covers off Miranda. That's unkind."

"I think we'd better go now," said Roger, "or Miss Pepper will be ringing up the village policeman."

"I'll come down with you," said Barney. "Then I'll leave the veranda door unlocked and unbolted as you suggested, Roger. Nobody will ever know it's open. It's obvious that no one ever comes here."

He saw them safely through the veranda door, Miranda sitting on his shoulder, wearing a doll's hat she had found. She fancied herself in it very much, and wore it back to front. Diana ran across the spidery veranda and down the steps to the wet grass.

The three of them got very wet going home through the thick undergrowth. Everything was dripping with silvery raindrops. The sun was trying to struggle out now. It might be quite a nice evening.

Miss Pepper was very concerned about them when they came in. "Oh, dear – how wet you are!" she said. "Go and put on something dry at once. I do hope you sheltered during the storm."

"Oh, yes," said Roger. But they didn't tell her where! No – that was their own very private secret. Nobody was going to know what they had been up to that afternoon.

When they went to bed that night the three called cautiously to one another, with Loony rushing as usual out of one bedroom and into another, sending all the mats sliding this way and that.

"Do you suppose Barney's in bed? Do you think he's all right?"

"I wouldn't like to sleep in that awful old deserted house at night!" That was Diana, of course.

"I bet he's in that bed and sound asleep! I bet he'll sleep sound till the morning!"

Barney *was* in bed and asleep. Miranda was in her little doll's bed. She usually slept with Barney, cuddled up to him, but the bed appealed to her funny little monkey mind very much. She was there, under the blanket, hugging the old doll.

Barney slept soundly till half past two in the morning and then he awoke with a jump! Miranda had leaped on top of him, and was cuddling into his neck, trembling,

chattering in a tiny voice in his ear.

Barney sat up.

"What's the matter, Miranda? What's frightened you? You're shivering all over. Were you lonely?"

Miranda clung to him and showed no signs of going back to her own little bed. Barney came to the conclusion that something had frightened her badly. But what? Was it a noise? It couldn't have been anybody coming into the nursery, because there was nobody to come!

He thought he heard a far-away sound then. He sat there on the bed, and listened, feeling his ears pricking up like a dog's. Was that a sound? Or was it his imagination?

It must be his imagination! He lay down again, with Miranda still cuddled into his neck – and then he sat up straight in one quick movement.

He *had* heard a sound! Quite a loud one. *Bang!* He listened intently, and heard it again.

Bang! Then the wind blew in at the window, and the ivy rustled against the glass. It made Barney jump. He realised what the rustling noise was at once – the wind in the ivy. Could the other noise have been caused by the wind too? Was it a door banging somewhere? Or was it perhaps the veranda door that had swung open in the wind and was banging?

Barney debated whether to go and see. He wasn't afraid, but he definitely didn't want to get up in the middle of a dark night and go wandering down dark stairs and along dusty passages without a light.

"If I hear the noise again I'll go down," he decided. "If I don't, I won't. I bet it's that beastly veranda door banging. I can't have shut it tightly enough."

He heard no more noises at all, except that the wind blew an old ivy leaf into the room and made it shuffle along the floor in a very hair-raising manner. For a moment poor Barney thought somebody was in the room but Miranda knew it was only a leaf, and didn't move. So Barney decided it was just something being blown along the floor.

He lay down again and shut his eyes. He listened for a few minutes longer, but all he heard was the monkey's little heart pattering fast against his neck.

Then he fell fast asleep and didn't wake till the sun pushed through the ivy leaves in the morning.

12

Mr King Arrives

Immediately after breakfast the next morning Diana wanted to go and see if Barney was all right.

"You've got to help make the beds and clear away the breakfast," said Roger. "We'll let Snubby go with Loony. I'm just about fed up with Snubby this morning. He put a worm in each of my shoes and put treacle or something on my sponge. If it's going to be one of his tiresome days we'd be better off without him. Let him go and plague Barney. Barney will know how to deal with him."

So Snubby was told to take some bread and butter and tomatoes and a bottle of milk to Barney. He set off in glee, Loony running at his heels.

He had got halfway over the grounds when he discovered that Loony was carrying Miss Pepper's hairbrush. So back he went and stood beneath Miss Pepper's window. He threw the brush up and it went straight in at the window.

There was an agonised yell and Snubby took to his heels. "Well, how was I to know she was standing in the way?" he argued to himself. "Just like a woman."

He looked down at Loony, who was again at his heels. This time he was carrying Mrs Round's old shoe-cleaning brush. Snubby stopped and addressed Loony fiercely.

"What do you think you're doing? Do you suppose I'm going to spend half the day taking back your silly brushes? You're a very bad dog. Take it back! Grrrrrr!"

Loony stared up at Snubby out of melting brown eyes, his tail down.

"Take it back! Don't you understand plain English when it's spoken?" yelled Snubby. "*Take it back!*"

Loony wagged his tail and darted off. Snubby was pleased. "Clever dog that," he said to a couple of sparrows nearby. "Understands every word I say."

He petted Loony when the dog came back. "Good dog. Took it all the way back to the kitchen and dropped it at Roundy's feet, I bet! Cleverest dog in the world."

Loony was very pleased. He had just dropped the brush down the nearest rabbit-hole. Well, if Snubby was so delighted with him, he'd drop plenty of other things down the rabbit-hole too.

The two went on together, Loony making a dart at anything that dared to move – a leaf, a swirl of dust, a bit of paper. Grrrrrr! He darted at Snubby's shoelaces, tripping him up. He behaved, in fact, just like the lunatic dog he was, and pleased Snubby very much indeed.

Snubby got to the old house at last and made his way round to the veranda. The door was fast shut. He pushed against it. It was so hard to open that he had to put down the basket he was carrying and push against the door with all his might. It obliged him by suddenly flying open and sending him headlong into the room. He sat down abruptly. Loony flung himself on him and licked him wildly.

"Hello! It's you, is it?" said Barney's voice. "I heard an awful row and came to see what it was. You're early. But why sit on that dusty floor?"

"Get off, Loony," said Snubby, pushing the excited spaniel away. He looked up at a Barney and grinned. "I found the door shut so hard I couldn't get in. So I had to barge against it with all my might and it flew open unexpectedly. And I flew in!"

"I see," said Barney. He spotted the basket outside. "I say – anything to eat? How super! Bread and butter and tomatoes! Are they for me?"

"Of course," said Snubby, getting up off

the dusty floor and brushing himself down. Barney took the basket into the room and shut the door. He pulled at it when he had shut it. It certainly did shut very tightly indeed. He looked puzzled.

"What's up?" said Snubby, noticing Barney's looks. "Anything wrong with the door?"

Barney told Snubby how frightened Miranda had been the night before, and how he had heard noises.

"I thought it must be the wind blowing open this door and banging it again," he said. "But I don't think it was now. The door fits so tightly."

They went up to the top rooms together. Snubby felt a little nervous. "I'd have hated that," he said to Barney. "Lying up there in the dark, hearing noises and not be able to put a light on. Brrr!"

"You might lend me your torch for tonight," Barney said. "I could do a little snooping round then, if I hear any more noises."

Snubby handed out his torch at once. He sat and watched Barney eat. "It's a gorgeous day," he said. "What about going to the river and getting a boat?"

"Yes, I'd like that," said Barney. "When do you start this tutoring of yours? Monday? We'd better make the most of our time then. I've been reading that play Roger lent me, this morning, up there in bed. It's great."

"Well, rather you than me," said Snubby, making a face. "I could never make out why Shakespeare wanted to write in such a funny way – you know, all the lines the same length. Seems a strange idea."

Barney laughed. "I wish I could come and listen to you all being taught," he said. "I bet I would enjoy it! I bet I'd learn a lot."

"Well!" Snubby looked at Barney as if he were quite mad. "You must be crazy. Fancy wanting to come and be taught! Well! – I don't see why you shouldn't come and listen if you want to. But fancy wanting to! Do you hear that, Loony. Here's a chap madder than you are!"

They walked to the door, their footsteps showing clearly in the dust. All their footmarks were there, Loony's as well. Snubby pointed them out.

"There's Loony's marks and mine, and these must be yours. Those are Di's, they're small. And there are Roger's – he's got the biggest feet of the lot."

They went out of the veranda door and Barney pulled it fast behind him. He pushed at it. It didn't open. He had to barge against it hard before it flew open. It couldn't have been this door banging last night. He must find out which door it was – if it was a door. It was a bit of a mystery!

Barney didn't sleep in the old house for a night or two after that. It was suddenly very hot weather again and the children hired a boat for a couple of days. Barney had the idea of sleeping in the boat, with a rug over him, and the boat-cushions for a bed.

"Do you mind if I do?" he asked the others. "It will save you the bother of taking it back to the boatman and I should love to bob about all night long on the water."

"Right," said Roger, pleased. "You do that. It's very stuffy up in those dusty old rooms in this weather – much better to sleep out if it's going to be hot and dry."

Monday came all too soon, and with it came Mr King, armed with textbooks and a suitcase. He was apparently going to stay at Rockingdown Cottage! The children hadn't realised this. They were shocked.

"Gracious! Have we got to have him for meals and everything?" said Snubby, dismally, seeing him go upstairs to one of the rooms on the first floor, accompanied by Mrs Round and Loony.

"Oh, don't be silly, Snubby," said Miss Pepper, impatiently. "He lives too far away to come over every day. And I may have to go away for a day or two, so I shall be glad to know there's someone responsible in the house to see to you."

A gloom settled on the children. Barney peeped in at the window and raised his eyebrows at them.

"Yes. He's come," said Diana. "*And* he's living here. Isn't that frightful? We shall have to behave more than ever."

"Well, I shan't," said Snubby.

"You never do," said Diana. "Barney, do you really want to come in and listen to us being tutored? Honestly, you'll be bored stiff. Honestly!"

Barney nodded. Travelling with the shows and circuses meant that he had not had the chance of a proper education and now he had a real thirst for book knowledge. He thought the three children very lucky in their education and their possession of so many books.

"All right. You come and knock at the door in about ten minutes time," said Diana. "Then when you come in you can be surprised to see us all working so quietly and . . ."

"He can apologise and back out," said Roger, enjoying this little plan. "And I'll say, 'Oh Mr King, would you mind if Barney sits here and waits for us?' And everything will be okay."

"Right," said Barney, and disappeared with Miranda just as Miss Pepper came into the study with Mr King.

"Ha! All ready and waiting, I see," said

Mr King. "Very good. We'll just see what standard you've all reached and then I can tell how to proceed with you."

In about a quarter of an hour's time Barney wandered past the window. He walked in through the open hall door and came to the study door. He knocked.

"Come in," yelled all the children at once, before Mr King could say a word. In came Barney, looking unexpectedly tidy, his hair wet and brushed back, and his hands and face clean.

"Oh – er? I'm sorry," he said, as he saw the three children sitting with Mr King at the table. "I don't want to interrupt. So sorry, sir."

He began to back out of the room, looking hot and bothered. Diana thought he was doing it all very well! Snubby choked back a giggle. Roger spoke earnestly to Mr King.

"Oh, Mr King – would you very much mind if our friend Barnabas sits down and waits for us?" he said. "He won't be any trouble."

"Certainly," said Mr King graciously. "By all means. Sit down by the window, Barnabas. Have you a book to read?"

Mr King was pleasantly surprised to see that Barney had a book of Shakespeare's plays. He turned his back on the boy and went on with his tutoring. Loony was lying quietly at Snubby's feet, rather exhausted by a mad race he had had up and down the stairs. Mr King congratulated himself on a nice quiet class. Miss Pepper had warned him he might not find things too easy, but nothing could be easier than this.

Snubby wondered where Miranda was. Barney hadn't brought her in. He must have shut her up somewhere – probably in the shed. He yawned. Things were getting boring. Even Loony was subdued.

Then things happened quickly! The door was slightly ajar and Miranda came shuffling in quietly. She saw Loony lying under the table asleep. Unseen by anyone, she went under Snubby's chair and came to the spaniel. Ha – her enemy was asleep! She took hold of both his long, floppy ears and pulled them hard, making a loud squawk as

she did so. Loony woke up in a hurry and yelped madly. He leaped out from under the table and snapped at Miranda, who hung on to the tablecloth to get out of his way. The cloth slid to the side and books fell off with a crash.

Then a battle royal developed under and round the table, and Mr King leaped up in alarm, his chair falling on Miranda, who happened to be chasing round it. She gave a howl and leaped on to his shoulder, pulling his ear hard.

Snubby rushed after Loony, who by now had fallen into the fireplace, bringing the tongs and the shovel down on himself with a clatter and almost leaping up the chimney in fright. Barney yelled at Miranda.

Snubby knocked a vase over as he tore after Loony, and Miss Pepper and Mrs Round, talking about meals in the kitchen, looked at each other in complete amazement as they listened to all the noise.

"What can they be doing?" said Miss Pepper and rushed to the study door, to be met by a crazy spaniel and an equally crazy monkey, both intent on devouring one another if they possibly could.

Miranda disappeared upstairs and hid. Loony crept back to Snubby, who had yelled at him without ceasing, partly to get him to come, and partly to make as much noise as he could.

"Well!" said Miss Pepper, annoyed. "I suppose this is what comes of letting Loony be in the room with you, Snubby."

"It was nothing to do with Loony," said Snubby indignantly. "He was asleep under the table. It was Miranda."

"Er – I think – I think you must take the dog out of the room," said Mr King, trying to recover himself under the prim, disapproving eye of Miss Pepper.

"But I tell you, it wasn't Loony's fault," almost yelled Snubby. "That's not fair."

"I cannot have either a dog or a monkey in my class," said Mr King with great dignity and sudden firmness. "They've both had a trial. It was not successful."

"But Mr King, Loony was fast asleep," wailed Snubby. "Didn't you hear his little snores?"

"No, I didn't," said Mr King. "Take the dog out, Peter."

Snubby took Loony by the collar to lead him out. He faced Mr King, his face as red as a beetroot.

"All right," he said, in a choking voice. "If you don't like my dog, I don't like you. You'll be sorry you didn't give him a chance – when he was fast asleep too!"

He went outside with Loony, who was quite scared now. Miss Pepper took him from Snubby. "Now don't be so silly, Snubby," she said. "Acting like a seven-year-old. I'll take Loony to the kitchen with Mrs Round."

"I'll pay Mr King back," said Snubby, darkly. "See if I don't. He'll be sorry, Miss Pepper. He will, really!"

13

Snubby Gets a Surprise

Mr King didn't like the next few days very much. Snubby produced his vast collection of tricks and became a perfect nightmare to the tutor.

Poor Mr King was given a rubber that wouldn't rub out but made strange yellow marks on the paper. He was provided with a ruler that was mysteriously wrong in its measurements and astonished him considerably. This ruler was one of Snubby's pet tricks, and had been confiscated at school, times without number, by irritated masters. But somehow or other it always found its way back to Snubby.

Books fell suddenly to the floor in a cascade, though Snubby was quite a long way from them. Mr King did not see the cunningly laid string that tipped up the bottom book when pulled, and sent the whole pile crashing down near him. The wall blackboard continually fell down in a most amazing way, and when Snubby was sent to clean it, a thick cloud of horrible-smelling dust appeared. It would have been a good thing if Mr King had examined Snubby's duster occasionally, but he didn't seem to think of things like that.

"Considering he's been a master in a boys' school he's pretty innocent," said Roger, who was very amused at all Snubby's idiotic tricks. As for Barney, he couldn't contain himself when Snubby perpetrated yet another foolish joke, and his uproarious laugh sounded all over the house.

Barney seemed to be the only one who really enjoyed the morning lessons. He didn't actually join the class but sat in the window, apparently reading. Mr King's back was to him, so he was unaware that the boy was absorbing everything that went on – listening to the explanations of mathematical problems, taking in the French lessons, enjoying the readings of English literature. There was nothing that Barney didn't enjoy. He had an extraordinary memory, and quite annoyed Roger by the way he could repeat the Latin phrases and declensions, when poor Roger himself was struggling to do the work that Mr King gave them.

Mr King was not really a very good teacher, Diana thought. He didn't seem interested enough. Nor could he keep Snubby in his place, but often seemed inclined to be amused at his silly tricks.

Snubby sulked. He hated Loony being kept away from him, and he was determined not to have Miranda sneaking in at any time. The little monkey was shut up in the shed while lessons were going on, but she sometimes managed to escape. She would find some crack or crevice and squeeze miraculously out of it – then she would appear silently at the window.

She would look for Loony, and then cuddle down with Barney. But at once Snubby would point her out to Mr King. "There's Miranda, Mr King. Can I get Loony in here?"

And Miranda would then have to go. Barney didn't bear any resentment toward Snubby for this. He liked the red-haired, freckled little pest, and always watched for his next trick.

Mr King was with the children in the mornings, and had all his meals with them, but he disappeared for the rest of the time.

"You're awfully fond of walking, aren't you?" Roger said, one afternoon, when Mr King set off with his stick and a book. "Where do you go?"

"Oh, anywhere," said Mr King vaguely. "Down to the river – through the village – and yesterday I visited that strange old mansion."

The children pricked up their ears at once. Would he discover their secret? Would he see the curtained windows they had seen, and notice the marks of their feet on the ground below?

"It's a very desolate place, I believe," said Diana, after a pause. "Not really worth looking at!"

"I thought it was very interesting," said Mr King. "It's very old – has quite a history. I wish I could go over it."

This was worse than ever. Had they better lock and bolt the veranda door in case Mr King found out that it could be opened? What a nuisance he was!

But if they did that they wouldn't be able to go in and out themselves if they wanted to – and as Barney was once more sleeping up in the nursery at the top of the old house it was useful to have the door left unlocked, so that they could use it if they wanted to.

By now Barney was quite used to sleeping in the old bed up in the little bedroom off the nursery. Diana had provided him with a garden cushion for a pillow, and found an old rug for him. He had taken some of the nursery crockery for himself.

Diana had managed to get rid of most of the dust and Barney enjoyed his little hiding-place. Nobody would ever guess he was there!

On wet days the children went up to the three rooms and amused themselves there.

They had once thought of playing hide-and-seek, using the front stairs and the back ones – but somehow it didn't work. Nobody liked hiding in the gloomy old place, and it was horrid tiptoeing along to find the hiders!

"I feel as if somebody is going to jump out and grab me all the time!" said Diana, with a shiver.

Barney had not heard any more noises. Miranda would not sleep in the doll's bed any more since she had been frightened the first night, but cuddled up with him. She only went into the doll's bed in the daytime when she got bored with the children's games. Then she would leap in, draw the bedclothes over her, and apparently sleep soundly with the old doll!

The only one who had really thoroughly explored the house and gone into every cupboard and corner was Loony, of course. His paw-marks were everywhere! He sniffed here and snuffled there, choking with the dust, and scraping madly at doors to make them open.

One night Snubby thought of going to sleep at the old house with Barney. The idea just came into his head.

"But why?" said Diana. "What a horrible idea! In that dark old place – I wouldn't sleep there for anything."

"I'd like to," said Snubby obstinately.

"Anything for a bit of a change. I call these hols too dull for words."

So that night, when he was supposed to be in bed and asleep, Snubby dressed again, and went out on the landing and listened. Downstairs the clock struck half past eleven. Was Mr King in bed? He usually went up at eleven, about the same time as Miss Pepper. Mrs Round didn't sleep in the house. She came in from the village each day.

Diana and Roger knew that Snubby was going to go to Barney for the night of course – but they hadn't bothered to keep awake to see him go. Snubby had borrowed Roger's torch because he had lent Barney his. He switched it on and off while he stood on the landing, to see if it worked all right. Yes, it did. It was a good torch, better than Snubby's.

Loony was at the boy's heels, his tail wagging. He liked this kind of thing. He pressed against Snubby's legs and didn't make a sound. He could be quiet and good if he wanted to – and he wanted to now, in case Snubby left him behind.

Snubby decided that Mr King was safely in bed. Anyway, in case he wasn't he'd go down the little back stairs. Then nobody would hear him. He crept to where they began and went down on tiptoe. He knew that the third and the seventh and the thirteenth stair creaked, so he counted them

132

carefully, and missed those out. He had his hand on Loony's collar to stop him tearing downstairs as he usually did.

Now he was at the bottom. Good. He cautiously opened the back door and looked out. It was a fine, starry night. There was no moon, but the stars were so bright that it was possible to see the trees outlined against the sky. Now for the walk across to Rockingdown Hall. The children had made quite a path of their own by now by hacking away branches and bushes.

Silently Snubby shut the door behind him and then he and Loony began their walk across the grounds. He could soon see the black mass of the old mansion looming up against the starry sky. It looked much bigger than it did in the daytime.

Loony made several little excursions into the undergrowth, and scared a good many rabbits who were not expecting him at all. He would have liked to chase them, but he wanted to keep with Snubby. It was night-time, and his master must be protected – against what, Loony didn't know. He just felt that he must keep close to him.

Snubby whistled softly. He wasn't scared but he felt it would be nice to whistle a little tune. He came out on to what had once been a great lawn and then he stopped very suddenly indeed, and his hand closed over Loony's collar.

He crouched down, holding Loony firmly. He could see a light moving near the house! He screwed up his eyes and tried to see what the light was. It must be the light of a torch! It moved here and there as if the owner were looking for something. Was it Barney? Snubby didn't like to whistle and find out, in case it wasn't.

And then Loony told him quite plainly that it wasn't Barney. He growled ominously, deep down in his throat. Snubby shook him a little to make him stop. He didn't want the person with the torch to know he was there with the spaniel. Loony would never growl at Barney; Snubby knew that. This was a stranger then. Whatever could he be doing? Or was he a tramp, seeking a way to get a night's shelter?

Snubby crept nearer with Loony. The dog now knew he was to keep quiet, and Snubby relaxed his hold on his collar. He had switched off his own torch. He followed the light of the other torch. Whoever held it was going systematically round the house, examining doors and windows. Suppose he came to the veranda door and found it open? Would he go in?

The man went round a corner of the house and Snubby saw his outline clearly. He gazed in real amazement. Why, he knew who this night prowler was. Surely it was Mr King!

14

A Mysterious Night

Snubby was full of astonishment. What in the world was Mr King doing prowling round the old house in the middle of the night, when he was supposed to be in bed? He stood still in the shadow of a big bush and thought about it. He couldn't make head or tail of it at all.

He made up his mind to make his way to the veranda door, go in as quietly as he could and run upstairs to warn Barney. He would lock the door behind him, so that Mr King couldn't get in. The man was now on the opposite side of the house to the veranda, the north side. If Snubby was quick he could get in without being seen or heard. He set off quietly for the house with Loony padding at his heels.

On to the veranda he crept, and had to put on his torch to see the handle of the door. He turned it and pushed. The door was easier to open now that the children had used it a good deal, and it swung inwards without much noise. Snubby went in with Loony and shut the door behind him. He shot the bolts and locked the door as well. Now Mr King wouldn't be able to get in!

He tiptoed across the hall and across into another room, standing by the door to see if he could spot Mr King's torch shining on the opposite side of the house. Yes, there it was!

Snubby shot upstairs to the first landing, then up again to the second. He went to the door that led into the passage to the nursery. He turned the handle.

The door was locked! Snubby was puzzled. Why was the door locked? Barney usually left it unlocked so that the children could go in and out as they pleased. He rattled the door gently. Then he heard Miranda chattering softly on the other side.

"Miranda," he said, in a low voice. "Where's Barney? Fetch Barney."

The door was unlocked immediately and Barney stood there with Miranda on his shoulder. He pulled Snubby into the passage and locked the door. In silence he led the way to the room where he slept.

"Why did you lock the door?" whispered Snubby.

"Because there's somebody about," said Barney in a low voice. "Didn't you bump into him?"

"Yes, almost! I know who it is, too," said Snubby.

"Who?" said Barney.

"Mr King!" said Snubby. "Yes – that's surprising isn't it? But it is. He's snooping all round the house trying to get in, I should think."

"Miranda woke me up a few minutes ago," said Barney. "I knew there was something up the way she was chattering and pawing at me, patting me on the cheek and putting her paw down my neck. So I got up and looked out of the window and I saw someone down below, using a torch!"

"Why didn't you rush down and lock the veranda door?" asked Snubby.

"Because I thought this fellow would have been at the door just about the same time as I would," said Barney. "So I locked the passage door instead. Then you came along, and I got a bit of a fright. I thought you must be the man – or another man perhaps. It was only when Miranda here began her friendly little chatter that I guessed it was one of you three. Are the others here? Why have you come tonight?"

Snubby explained in whispers. "The others are in bed. I just had a sudden idea I'd like a bit of an adventure so I came along to spend the night with you and I saw this man just as I came up to the house. I was awfully surprised when I saw who it was."

"What do you suppose he's doing?" said Barney, puzzled. "What's he after?"

"Can't imagine," said Snubby. "By the way, have you heard any more noises in the night, Barney?"

"None," said Barney. "I think it must just have been the wind banging the door, that's all."

He went to the window and looked out cautiously. There was nothing to be seen. "He may be at the other side of the house," said Barney. "Well, now that the veranda door is safely locked we know he can't get in. Let's go down the passage, unlock the door there, and see if we can find out where Mr King is now."

Off they went, very quietly. Miranda was once more on Barney's shoulder, chattering softly in a whispery voice. Loony trotted along with them, enjoying himself.

They unlocked the passage door and went down the stairs quietly to the rooms on the next floor. There was one with a bay window that jutted out – they would stand in the bay and see if they could spot Mr King's torchlight. They spotted it at once, moving slowly along below, as if he were examining every window catch. What was he doing? Why did he want to get in?

And then, just as they stood there quietly watching, they heard a noise.

Bang! Thud! Thud! Bang!

They almost jumped out of their skins. Evidently Mr King heard the noise too, for he switched off his torch at once. Snubby clutched Barney in fright. Loony growled loudly and Miranda sat quite still, listening.

"That's the noise I heard the first night," said Barney in a low voice. "Is it a door banging, do you think?"

"Well, it might be," said Snubby, listening. "I don't know."

Bang!

"There it is again," said Barney. "Where is the noise coming from?"

"Downstairs," said Snubby, his teeth beginning to chatter. He was ashamed of himself for being afraid, and tried to shut his mouth firmly to stop his teeth from behaving in such an idiotic way. He badly wanted to go upstairs again and lock the passage door and go into the nursery and lock that door too! He was shocked to find that he wasn't nearly as brave as he as always thought he was.

Barney was quite calm and didn't seem afraid at all. He stood there listening. The noises came again. Yes – they were definitely from downstairs.

There was no sign of Mr King's torch. Either he was in hiding or he had gone – or had he joined the persons who were making the noise? Barney thought it was very likely that that was the reason he had come along that night, to join friends of his somewhere about here!

He stood there, puzzling it out, waiting for more noises. There came a curious whining, half-screeching noise that made all Snubby's hair slowly stand upright on his head, much to his surprise – and then dead silence. Not a bang or a thud came again.

"Well," said Barney at last, moving from the window, "I think the show's over for tonight, whatever it was! Mr King's disappeared, and the noises off have stopped. Let's go and explore downstairs and see if we can find out what made them."

Snubby was horrified. What! Go down in the dark and snoop about to see what made those terrifying noises? Barney must be mad. He clutched his arm.

"No, Barney! Let's go upstairs and lock ourselves in!"

"You go," said Barney. "Take Loony with you. I'll go and explore myself."

But poor Snubby didn't dare to go upstairs by himself – no, not even with Loony at his heels! He thought that of the two evils, going with Barney was the lesser; he couldn't possibly go anywhere by himself at the moment!

Feeling very panicky, Snubby went down the stairs with Barney. Loony pressed against his heels and that was comforting. Snubby wished he were a dog too. Dogs never seemed really afraid!

"I think the noises came from the kitchen part," said Barney, in a whisper. "Let's just stand here in the hall and listen once more."

They stood there, and then, to Snubby's horror, something touched his hair! He almost yelled in fright. Then the something pulled his hair – and Snubby nearly died with relief. It was only Miranda putting out her paw from where she sat on Barney's shoulder, and being affectionate!

They went into the great kitchens. Barney switched on his torch and the beam played over the room in front of them. Shadows seemed to flee into the corners as the beam of light moved round the room. Snubby trembled and Barney felt him.

"You frightened?" he said in surprise. "Don't worry, Snubby. Miranda and Loony would soon let us know if there was anyone near. There can't be anyone about now or Miranda would chatter and Loony would growl."

That was true. Snubby felt relieved at once. There was nothing to be seen in the great kitchens at all. The beam of light travelled over the floor and showed footmarks – but only those of the children and the dog, where they had only gone across the rooms. No other footsteps showed at all.

"Nobody has been here," whispered Barney and he went into the scullery. This was a big room with a pump for water as well as taps in a sink. Nobody had been there either. Not even the children's footsteps showed here in the dust on the floor. They had never been into the scullery. It was very puzzling. How could people make loud noises downstairs and yet leave no footmarks or any sign of having been there?

"It's a bit spooky, isn't it?" said Snubby at last. Barney laughed.

"Don't you believe it! Those noises were made by people – there was nothing spooky about them. Surely you don't believe in spooks! What a baby you are!"

"Well, it's all rather funny," said Snubby. "All those noises and nothing to show for it. Not even a footmark! Can you tell me how anyone could make such a row down here and yet not leave the dust disturbed?"

"No, I can't," said Barney. "But I'm going to find out! That's quite certain. There's something very strange about all this and I'm going to solve the mystery!"

"Do you think Mr King's in it, whatever it is?" asked Snubby.

Barney considered. "I shouldn't be surprised," he said. "Ask him a few questions tomorrow, Snubby, and see what he says. Ask him if he slept well – ask him if he heard any noises in the night – ask him if he ever walks in his sleep!"

Snubby grinned in the dark. "Right! I'll just see what he says! I say, is the show really over now, Barney? I'm frightfully sleepy."

"Yes, it seems to be over," said Barney. "Come on, Miranda – to bed! Are you really going to sleep here tonight, Snubby?"

"Well, nothing would make me go back to Rockingdown Cottage in the dark tonight," said Snubby. "Can you make room on your bed for me?"

"I suppose that means Loony too!" said Barney. "Yes, I expect the bed will take four of us. Come on!"

They went upstairs again, carefully locking the passage door and the nursery doors, and went into the little third room. Snubby felt sure it would take him ages to get to sleep but his eyes shut tight as soon as his head was on the pillow. And there the four of them slept soundly till the morning, Miranda cuddled in Barney's neck and Loony on Snubby's feet. What a bedful!

15

Snubby is a Nuisance

Snubby was up and about very early, anxious to be back at the cottage before anyone else was up. Barney went with him and sat in the tumbledown summerhouse. Snubby promised to see if he could manage to smuggle him out some breakfast.

But Mrs Round caught sight of Miranda outside the summerhouse as she hurried to the cottage to do her morning work and get breakfast. She peeped in and saw Barney.

"Ah, another one to breakfast, I suppose!" she said. Barney grinned. He and Mrs Round understood one another. He had done little odd jobs for her – unstopping her sink when it got stopped up, putting up a new clothesline for her and so on. She thought he was a very handy, obliging boy, though she couldn't bear Miranda.

Barney had breakfast with everyone else. Miss Pepper didn't mind. One more didn't make much difference, and Barney seemed a nice boy, if a little strange. Mr King was there too, looking a little tired. He came in very late for breakfast.

Snubby was ready and waiting for him. He had told Diana and Roger the happenings of the night before, and they had listened, thrilled and astonished.

"Lucky fellow, having all that fun with Barney in the middle of the night!" said Roger. Snubby didn't tell him how frightened he had been. Now that it was daylight and the sun was shining brilliantly he quite forgot how his teeth chattered and his hair had stood on end.

He was boastful and brave now – he had had a marvellous night while the others had been fast asleep in bed!

They had been amazed to hear that Mr King had been on the prowl in the night too. Roger whistled. "What on earth was he up to? He's a dark horse, isn't he? Why didn't he say anything about it?"

Mr King made his apologies for coming late to breakfast and helped himself to cornflakes. Snubby began at once.

"Did you have a bad night, Mr King?"

Mr King looked surprised at this concern on Snubby's part. "No," he said. "I had a very good one thank you."

"I didn't," said Snubby. "I was awake a lot. Didn't you hear noises in the night?"

Mr King looked rather startled. He glanced at the innocent-looking Snubby.

"What noises?" he said, cautiously.

"Oh, just noises," said Snubby. "Perhaps you slept too well to hear anything, Mr King."

"I certainly slept very well – in fact, as you know, I overslept," said Mr King. "Miss Pepper, will you have some mustard?"

Snubby wasn't going to have the subject changed like that. He persisted with his questions. "I thought I heard somebody about last night. It might have been somebody walking in their sleep. Do you ever walk in your sleep, Mr King?"

"Never," said Mr King, shortly. "These are very nice sausages, Miss Pepper."

"I wonder who it was getting up in the night," said Snubby, innocently. "Did you, Roger? Did you, Diana?"

"We didn't," said Roger and Diana, enjoying all this baiting of poor Mr King.

"And you didn't either, did you, Mr King?" said Snubby, turning to him. "Unless you were walking in your sleep, of course."

"I've already told you I don't walk in my sleep," said Mr King, exasperated. "Now, will you kindly let me talk to Miss Pepper? If this is your latest idea of being funny, think of something else. It's puerile."

"What's puerile?" said Snubby at once.

"I'll tell you in your Latin lesson," said Mr King, in a voice that promised a very harassing lesson for Snubby that morning.

"Though I should have thought you already knew what *puer* meant. It's a pity you're so behind."

Snubby winked at the others. He had found out what he wanted to know. Mr King wasn't going to admit that he had been out last night, that was evidently his own business. He was going to keep it a secret which probably meant he was going snooping again sometime. It would be fun to keep an eye on him in that case.

"Are you going for a walk today?" asked Snubby, addressing himself to Mr King again. "Can I come with you?"

"I am going for a walk, but I certainly don't want you with me in your present tiresome mood," said Mr King. Snubby at once made up his mind to follow him on his walk. Loony, who was under the table, quietly began to chew Mr King's shoelace. Miranda had been left in the shed in case she and Loony started one of their mad games with one another.

Snubby was even more tiresome in lessons than he had been at breakfast. He was told to make up three sentences and write them down in French. He produced the following sentences and read them out gleefully.

"*Ils étaient de bruits dans la nuit* – There were noises in the night.

"*Je me promene dans mon sommeil* – I walk in my sleep.

"*Je ne parle toujours le vrai* – I do not always speak the truth."

Mr King listened to these peculiar sentences in silence. He looked consideringly at Snubby and seemed about to break out angrily. Then he apparently changed his mind.

"Full of the most elementary mistakes," he said coldly. "Please write out three more. If those are also full of mistakes you can write out yet another three."

Snubby decided not to bait Mr King any more. He wrote three innocent French sentences which were perfectly correct in every way. This was not surprising as he had taken them from his French book. Mr King did not seem to be up to little tricks of this sort. Snubby wished fervently that his French master at school could be taken in so easily. Unfortunately Monsieur Rieu was apt to smell out a trick before it was even played.

After lunch the children met together in the summerhouse. They giggled when they talked about Snubby's cheekiness that morning.

"All the same, Mr King's pretty peculiar," said Roger. "Why all the secrecy about his prowling? He could easily have said that he couldn't sleep and went for a walk."

"I'm going to track him this afternoon," said Snubby. "Aren't we, Loony, old chap?"

Loony agreed eagerly, leaping up on Snubby's knee and licking his nose lavishly. He then tried to lie on his back, fell off with a bump, saw Miranda and raced after her till she bounded up a tree and sat there chattering at him.

"The names Miranda calls him!" said Barney, pretending to be shocked. "Wherever did she learn them!"

Mr King set off on his walk at half past two, taking with him a map and a stick. Snubby, who was on the watch, let him get a good way ahead and then went quietly after him. Loony, having been told to keep quiet, nosed along at his heels.

Mr King struck across country towards the river. Snubby was a little disappointed. He had hoped that he would go snooping round the old mansion again. If so he might possibly get in, as the veranda door was not locked. Most unfortunately the key would not lock it from the outside.

Snubby followed Mr King carefully, occasionally sinking down flat with Loony if the tutor stopped, or looked round. This caused great astonishment to an old lady who was near Snubby when he did one of his disappearing acts. He lay down flat, hissing to Loony to lie down too. The old lady went up in concern.

"Are you all right, little boy?" she said. "Do you feel ill?"

"Ssst!" said Snubby, annoyed. He crawled sideways into the hedge like a crab and the old lady looked at him in alarm. The boy must be mad. Then an idea came to her.

"Are you playing cowboys and Indians?" she asked.

Mr King had now walked on. Snubby got up cautiously and stalked down the other side of the hedge. "I'm Chief Redfeather," he said to the relieved old lady. "Be careful of my men. Don't let them scalp you, whatever you do!"

He left the old lady looking out for his "men", and went on after Mr King, frightening several cows by suddenly flattening himself out on the ground whenever Mr King stopped to consider his way. Snubby thoroughly enjoyed himself. He was getting his own back nicely on Mr King.

They came to the river eventually. Mr King glanced at his map again and then made his way up the river. There was a very wild part just there, and both Mr King and his pupil found the going difficult. In fact, Snubby, having fallen into a marshy piece two or three times, and having had to haul poor Loony out of the mud at least six times, almost gave up.

Steep hills now rose up on one side of the river. A stream came into it from the east, and to Snubby's surprise Mr King now left the main river and began to follow the

stream. Poor Snubby groaned. This was much worse than he had imagined. It must already be nearly teatime and there was all that way to go back!

To make matters worse, Mr King suddenly sat down on a nice dry spot, pulled out a packet from his pocket, and opened it, displaying a very fine array of sandwiches and cake! Snubby could have cried! Why hadn't he had the sense to find out if Mr King had meant to get back to tea or not?

He had to lie under a rather prickly bush and watch Mr King devour every sandwich and two pieces of Mrs Round's fruit cake. Loony whined when the smell wafted towards him on the wind. He thought his master was extremely foolish not to have brought something to eat too. Snubby saw Mr King raise his head when he heard the whine, and he hissed at the surprised spaniel.

"Shut up, idiot! Not a word!"

Loony looked at his master for a moment, made his mind up that Snubby was temporarily mad, and curled himself up in disgust to go to sleep. Snubby was very glad when Mr King folded up his sandwich papers and put them back into his pocket. Now perhaps he would go home!

But he didn't. He followed the stream instead, and Snubby had to give up the chase because the country was now too bare for him to follow without being seen. All that way for nothing!

Wait a minute, though. Mr King was standing still now, looking with great interest at something. What was it? Snubby was full of curiosity. He saw Mr King bend down to the stream and touch something. Then he bent very low, almost disappeared and remained practically out of sight for a few minutes. He then reappeared again, and took out some binoculars. He swept the countryside with them. What could he be looking for? And what had he found in the stream? Snubby made up his mind to go and see, even if it made him hours late for dinner!

16

Snubby is Not Very Clever

Mr King at last went off in another direction altogether, much to Snubby's surprise. He took a look at his map and set off to the south, across rough country – hilly country too. Snubby, who hadn't the faintest idea where he was, and felt that he was miles from home, looked after Mr King with exasperation.

"Now where's he going? What a wild-goose chase this is!"

He waited till Mr King was out of sight behind a small clump of trees and then went as quickly as he could to where he had seen him stop by the stream. There was a tiny creek there, a little backwater, with trees and bushes overhanging. Pulled right back in the creek, almost hidden under a bush, was a boat. It had no name. A couple of oars lay in it, and a coil of rope. Nothing else. How mysterious!

Snubby gazed at the lonely little boat. Who owned it? There didn't appear to be a house within miles. What a strange thing to leave a boat here, on this stream, hidden like that. Why? Who used it? And where did the owner live? Snubby wished he had binoculars like Mr King. Then he could have swept the countryside with them and found out if any cottage or house was hidden in any corner of the hills.

By the time he had finished examining the boat, which told him absolutely nothing, Mr King had completely disappeared. Snubby couldn't see a sign of him anywhere. He looked down at the patient spaniel.

"Could you track him, Loony, do you think?" he asked. "Then we could follow him without getting lost."

Loony looked up intelligently and wagged his tail. "All right, track him then," said Snubby, waving his hand vaguely in the direction in which Mr King had gone.

Loony started off eagerly, for all the world as if he knew what Snubby meant. Snubby was delighted.

"He's the cleverest dog that was ever born," he said to himself, as he followed after the pattering spaniel. But when Loony led him to eight rabbit-holes in succession, he began to change his mind.

"You're daft," he said to Loony gloomily. "Do you really think I said find rabbit-holes? Do use a little common sense, Loony."

Loony barked and wagged his tail, and started off to find yet another hole. But Snubby had had enough. He was tired, muddy, hungry and thirsty. In addition he felt most annoyed with Mr King. His tracking had taught him nothing except that Mr King liked long and apparently aimless walks and he had seen a hidden boat which didn't seem to belong to anyone at all. Mr King had had a good tea, and had now completely disappeared into the blue. Snubby would get lost if he tried to follow his trail. He must go back to the stream, follow it to the river, then follow the river to the part he knew, and so get home.

It seemed a long way to poor Snubby and even Loony's heart sank a little as they began to stumble back down the marshy bank of the little stream.

Snubby didn't arrive home till eight o'clock. He found everyone in a terrible state about him, even Mr King. He glared at the tutor, feeling that it was all his fault he had had such a terrible afternoon and evening.

"How long have you been back?" he asked.

"Oh, since about half past five," said Mr King, to Snubby's intense astonishment. Half past five! Why, Mr King had got back from the stream in about half an hour then – or less. But how had he done it? Snubby couldn't make it out at all. He was almost in tears with tiredness and hunger.

Miss Pepper suddenly took pity on him and forgot her worry and her anger over his being so late. She hustled him up to a hot bath and got him to bed, then she brought up a bowl of Mrs Round's delicious tomato soup, a plate of corned beef and salad and another bowl of fresh peaches and cream. Snubby was in the seventh heaven of delight. What a feast! Honestly, it was worth going through all those awful hours of hunger and thirst to get all this!

He said very little to Miss Pepper about his long absence. "I went for a walk and lost my way," he said. "That's all."

"Where did you go?" asked Mr King, curiously.

"I really don't know," said Snubby politely. "Where did you go?"

"Oh, round and about," said Mr King. "But I was sensible, I took my tea with me. Pity you didn't come across me, I could have shared it with you."

Snubby grinned to himself. Little did Mr King know that he had been hidden under a bush near enough to him to see what he ate! Not till Miss Pepper and Mr King had gone downstairs did Snubby tell the others exactly what had happened. They were very interested indeed.

"Fancy a boat there, hidden under the

trees, with no visible owner anywhere," said Roger. "A mystery!"

"Yes. But what seems to be much more mysterious is how did Mr King get back here so quickly?" said Snubby. "I mean, it took hours to get to that boat, you know, and yet it seems only to have taken Mr King under half an hour to get back home!"

"Well, he must have taken a short cut back," said Roger. "Let's have a squint at a map and find out."

He went downstairs, found a big map of the district, and put his finger on Rockingdown Village. "Here we are – here's the village, see – and there's the way to the river. Now you went up the river, you say, like that."

"Yes. And we came to a stream, quite a big one where it entered the river," said Snubby, stabbing a piece of corned beef with his fork. "Is the stream shown?"

"Yes, here it is – Rockingdown Stream," said Roger. "You say you went up it a good way – right, here we go," and he ran his finger up the stream.

Diana gave an exclamation. "Well, it's quite easy to see how Mr King got home so quickly! Look, he had walked almost round in a circle and by taking a short cut across this hill, he would have come out quite near Rockingdown Cottage. See – it's hardly any distance."

Diana was right. Because of the way the river curved, Snubby had walked in a half-circle, and then up the stream, which made a three-quarter circle, and the other quarter of the circle lay over the hill to Rockingdown Cottage. Easy!

Snubby let out a long sigh. "Gosh! I was certainly a prize idiot! There I was, only a little way from here, and I go and walk miles and miles the long way round. But I didn't know."

"You want to take a compass with you,"

said Roger. "Anyway, if you want us to see the boat, it won't take long to get there. We'll take this path here, and go over the hill, across this bit of marsh to the stream – and the boat will be somewhere there!"

It all looked very easy and simple, when the map lay before them. Snubby really felt exasperated when he saw what a long and unnecessary walk home he had had. What a lover of walking Mr King must be to struggle along through marshy ground and overgrown paths, up the stream! Well it was the last time he would ever do any tracking. Mr King could go walking every day if he wanted to – but as far as Snubby was concerned he would go alone!

Snubby fell asleep immediately after he had finished his supper. What with his disturbed night, and his long and tiresome walk, he was tired out. There were going to be no excursions for him tonight!

Barney played a game with Roger and Diana till it was time for them to go to bed. The map they had all been looking at lay unheeded on a nearby table.

Barney, who was out of the game for one or two turns, glanced idly at the map. His eye followed the stream, and he looked at it, puzzled.

"Here's a funny thing!" he said to the others, suddenly. "Look!"

"What?" said Diana, throwing the dice

out of the shaker. "A six – good! Just what I wanted."

"Look," went on Barney. "See this stream? The one where Snubby found the boat. Look where it goes."

They all looked. "Well, I don't see anything wonderful about it," said Roger. "It just runs close by Rockingdown Manor, then goes off northwards to those hills – where it apparently has its source."

"Yes, but don't you see," said Barney. "Have you ever seen any stream in the grounds at all? The old house is set right in the middle of very big grounds. Well, this map apparently shows the stream very close to the house indeed, but you know as well as I do that there is no stream to be found here in these grounds."

The others stopped their game and looked more closely. Yes, it certainly seemed as if the stream ran very close to the house indeed. The map was on a large scale and the stream was shown, or seemed to be shown, actually in the grounds.

And yet what Barney had said was quite true. None of them had seen any stream in the grounds at all, and yet they had explored them very thoroughly indeed.

Miranda dropped down on the map and they pushed her off. They were interested now. Where was the stream? They tried to figure it out.

"It's not near our cottage, that's certain. It's not anywhere near the village itself, or we'd have had to cross it over a bridge or something. It must be on the other side of the old house. We'll look and see."

"If it isn't it must simply have dried up or altered its course or something," said Roger.

"We can easily find out," said Barney.

"How?" asked Diana.

"Use your brains!" said Roger.

"Oh, of course, we can follow the stream all the way up from the river!" said Diana. "I never thought of that. How stupid of me!"

"Yes. We can easily follow it and see what its course is," said Barney. "Not that it matters really. I was just suddenly interested to notice how near it came to the old house when I was looking at the map."

The subject was dropped and a new game begun. Miss Pepper put her head in at the study after a while. "Barney, it's time you went. It's raining hard. Is it far for you to go to your lodgings?"

Miss Pepper thought Barney had lodgings somewhere. He had told her he had a room to sleep in and she imagined it was one in the village. Nobody undeceived her. They couldn't possibly tell her where Barney really slept.

"No. Not far, Miss Pepper," said Barney,

rising to go. He really had very good manners. "I'll be seeing you tomorrow," he said to Diana and Roger. "So long!"

He went off with Miranda as usual on his shoulder, Loony escorting him to the door, sending a few barks after him, which were really meant for Miranda. "Good riddance to bad rubbish!" was what his barks meant. Then back he trotted to the others, pleased with himself.

Barney went cautiously through the grounds, wondering if Mr King – or anybody else – was about. But he saw no one. All the same, he locked the veranda door and the passage door too; he didn't mean to be disturbed in the middle of the night again!

17

Barney Does Some Exploring

All the same, it was a very disturbing night for Barney. He was awakened suddenly by Miranda chattering to him in fright, pulling at his hair and ears. He took her in his arms and sat up in bed.

Bang! Thud!

There were the noises again. What was going on in this empty old house? Should he get up and see, or should he lie down and sleep again? There was nobody actually in the house, otherwise there would be strange footprints as well as their own.

The noises came again, followed by the strange whining half-screeching sound. Miranda was absolutely terrified. She tried to get inside Barney's shirt, and made little whining noises of fear. He comforted her automatically, listening hard. What was making those noises? And where were they being made? They simply must be inside the house!

Barney sighed. He was tired after his

disturbed night the night before, and he dearly wanted to go to sleep. But he felt intensely curious about all this. He was not in the least frightened, and he threw off the blanket and went across the room, feeling for the door. He did not put on the torch for fear of the light being seen by anyone who might perhaps be outside.

Miranda tried to pull him back. She leaped down to the floor and pulled at his legs, chattering wildly. Barney laughed.

"You'll be all right with me, Miranda. I'm not afraid! Don't be a little idiot. Now be quiet or you'll be heard."

He went down the passage and unlocked the door there quietly. He wondered how the person or persons who made the noises could possibly get into the house – and if they did where were the footmarks they made? He gave it up. It was a real puzzle.

"I'll solve it somehow though," thought Barney. "I don't know what's going on, but something is! And what's more, I believe Mr King's in it too, whatever it is. Maybe he can get into the house somewhere we haven't found and it's he who makes those extraordinary noises."

Thud! Thud! There it was again, deep down in the house. One thud was so loud that Barney was really startled.

He went right down to the kitchen, feeling his way cautiously, not daring to put on his torch. All was quiet there. Barney switched his torch on and off very swiftly, gazing at the floor as he did so. No fresh footprints were there, nobody had been in the kitchen.

He went to the scullery. No footprints there either. And yet it honestly seemed as if the noises came from this direction. As he stood there, waiting, a noise came again.

Thud! Thud! And then the whining sound, and an odd guttural noise that Barney hadn't heard before. He felt a moment's fear. That was a strange noise – what could it be? It didn't sound at all human. Could there be dungeons or something under the scullery floor? Was the house old enough for those? What about cellars? Where were they? There must be plenty in an old house of this kind.

Barney wondered why he hadn't thought of cellars before. They ought to be explored! Probably the explanation of the noises lay in the cellars.

He went through the scullery and came to some stone-paved outhouses – one was a washhouse, the other must have been a dairy at one time. It had shelves of marble all round to hold pans of cream.

His torch swung over the floor and the beam showed up dust again. Not a footprint anywhere! Not even Loony's. The doors to the outhouses had been shut, so Loony hadn't gone through them. Barney looked carefully over the floor. He found what he was seeking – a square place where a trapdoor lay, its handle sunk into a groove in the wood, so that no one would trip over it.

That's where the cellars would be, under there. Well, he wasn't going down there tonight. Whatever was going on could go on without him. Fearless as Barney was he had no wish to explore dark cellars at that moment – especially cellars that gave out such peculiar noises!

He would tell the children in the morning and they would all do a little exploring. It would be exciting! Barney went back to bed, yawning. A few more noises came up to him as he lay in bed but he took no notice of them. Miranda didn't either. She was cuddled up to him, half asleep, her tiny front paws round his neck.

In the morning Barney told the children what he had heard, and how he had gone into the outhouses and seen the trapdoor.

"The washhouse and the dairy open out on one side of the scullery," he said. "We've never been into them. There's a trapdoor in the dairy – I bet it leads down to the cellars. We'll explore there this afternoon. I'm sure there's something peculiar going on in there, though I can't for the life of me imagine what it is!"

This was so thrilling that nobody could

pay much attention to their tutoring that morning. Fortunately Mr King seemed a little bored with it too, and appeared to be working out calculations of his own on a sheet of paper.

Loony crept in unnoticed and lay at Snubby's feet. He began to gnaw the edge of the tablecloth that hung just by his nose. He made a kind of chewy noise and Mr King looked up.

"Stop making that silly noise, Snubby," he said. Snubby hastily kicked Loony to stop him chewing and there was peace again. Everyone was thankful when the morning came to an end. Mr King suddenly noticed with a start that Loony had apparently materialised under the table and was just about to make a stern remark about it, when Snubby fell on Loony and fondled him extravagantly.

"How did you know we'd just finished? How clever of you to come in at just the right moment! Mr King, wasn't he clever to know it was the right minute to come in?"

Mr King said nothing. He just looked sternly at Loony and even more sternly at Snubby. Before he could make up his mind exactly how to answer Snubby, the boy rushed from the room with Loony, yelling, "Come on, Loony, walkie-walks!"

The other three children grinned at one another. They had known perfectly well that

Loony was under the table all the morning and had wondered when Mr King would find out.

"Can Barney stay to lunch, Miss Pepper, can he, can he?" shouted Snubby, who always yelled at the top of his voice for about ten minutes after finishing his tutoring. "It's cold chicken and salad and Roundy says there is enough."

"All right, all right," said Miss Pepper, putting her hands over her ears. "Why must you shout so? And didn't I tell you to go upstairs after breakfast and change out of that disgustingly dirty shirt?"

"Oh, so you did," said Snubby. "Well, need I now? I shall probably get awfully dirty this afternoon."

"Why? What are you going to do?" asked Miss Pepper. "You came home filthy yesterday too. Is it necessary to do all the dirty things you seem to do?"

"Yes, it's absolutely necessary," Snubby assured her cheerfully. "Well, I won't change my shirt then. I don't want Roundy to have any more washing to do. I wish I was like Loony, and just wore my own coat of hair and nothing else."

"You wouldn't manage to keep yourself as clean as Loony does, even then," said Miss Pepper. "I really do think you are the most filthy dirty child I have ever—"

"Dear old Pep!" said the irrepressible

Snubby and swung her round, trying to dance with her.

She was half cross, half amused.

Mr King came in suddenly, looking as black as thunder. "Snubby! Did you tie that bit of string between the gateposts in the garden? I've almost broken my ankle over it. Miss Pepper, I think I need to buy a cane this afternoon -- a nice thin one that goes *wheeeee* in the air!"

"Do," said Miss Pepper. "Lend it to me to use some time will you?"

Snubby didn't like this. It wasn't good when Miss Pepper and Mr King both sided against him. "I'm sorry, Mr King. I was practising jumping. You must have fallen over my jumping-string."

"Snubby, that kind of thing is stupid and dangerous," said Miss Pepper. "I shall make you go without your pudding at lunch today. I've told you before about dangerous tricks. I will not have them played."

"Aha, no pudding for you, then," said Mr King, pleased. "Serves you right, you little pest."

Snubby lost his high spirits and looked sulky. He couldn't do anything if both Mr King and Miss Pepper were in league against him. There were all sorts of nasty punishments they could think up. He scowled at their retreating backs.

"I'll have to set them against one

another," he thought and sat down to work out a plan. It didn't take him long. He went into the kitchen and got the kitchen pepper-pot when Mrs Round's back was turned. He slipped it into his pocket. He tiptoed out again, Loony sniffing at his pocket. Then the spaniel suddenly sneezed.

"Pepper up your nose?" said Snubby, loudly, so that Miss Pepper could hear. "Poor little dog. Pepper's awful, isn't it?"

Lunch was soon ready. There were big bowls of steaming pea soup. Mrs Round was good at making soup, and she knew the children liked it.

Snubby had a few words with Roger, who grinned and nodded. They all sat down. Roger tasted his soup. "Wants salt and pepper," he said. "Pass the pepper, Di. Mr King, will you have some?"

Just as Mr King took up the pepper-pot to sprinkle a little on his soup, Snubby left his place and went to pick up his table napkin ring. As he passed behind the unsuspecting Mr King he whipped the kitchen pepper-pot from his pocket and tossed pepper round Mr King's head.

Miss Pepper didn't notice anything. Nor did poor Mr King. He finished sprinkling pepper and salt on his soup, and was about to take up his spoon when he felt an enormous sneeze coming. He hastily got out his handkerchief.

"Whooooosh-oo! I beg your pardon, Miss Pepper. A-whooooosh-oo! Oh dear me! Here's another one coming. Really – I – whooooosh-oo!"

Miss Pepper looked at him. What an extraordinary paroxysm of sneezing! Mr King was now purple in the face, wondering whether to leave the room or not.

"A-whooosh-ooosh-oo!" he began again. "I do apologise. It must be a little pepper up my nose!"

The children roared with laughter. Good

old Mr King! He had said the exact words that Miss Pepper hated.

Miss Pepper looked at Mr King coldly. How dare he make fun of her like this – in front of the children too. She didn't believe in his sneezes at all, now that he had said the fatal words. "Perhaps you would like to leave the room till your – er – indisposition is over?" she said, in an icy voice.

Mr King got up and went. The children heard him still coping with his sneezes in the bedroom above, and Diana was almost helpless with laughter. Every time she ate a mouthful of soup she laughed and choked. Miss Pepper got really angry.

"Now stop it, Diana. It's an old joke now and a silly one, this pepper joke. It's not even funny."

Snubby made his face solemn. "I think it was rude of Mr King to say that in front of you," he said righteously. "I mean – it's all very well for us to say silly things like that, Miss Pepper, but Mr King shouldn't forget his manners, should he?"

"That's enough," said Miss Pepper. "Not a word more from you. And when Mr King comes back we shall not refer to this again."

Mr King came back shortly looking very sheepish, not understanding his fit of sneezing at all. He was upset to find Miss Pepper so cold to him. Was she cross because of his sneezing at the table? Well, anybody might do that! Sneezes were like hiccups – you just couldn't stop them.

The meat course came in and then the pudding. Snubby was supposed to go without but because Miss Pepper was still annoyed with Mr King she quite forgot to leave Snubby out when she served the pudding, and he got his usual big helping.

And poor Mr King, who remembered about it, didn't dare to remind Miss Pepper! Snubby grinned. He had got on top as usual!

18

A Very Exciting Afternoon

The exploration that afternoon proved very interesting indeed. They all arrived at Rockingdown Manor at just after half past two, full of anticipation. What would they find in the cellar?

Snubby had forgotten his fears of a night or two ago. He was once again brave and fearless, entering the old house first of all, and even shouting loudly in it to make the echoes come.

Barney laughed at him. Snubby always amused him with his silly tricks and ridiculous ways. They all went to the big kitchen and out into the scullery, then through the door that led into the outhouses; the washhouse first and then the dairy with its marble shelves.

"Here we are," said Barney. "And look, there's the trapdoor. I bet that leads down into the cellars. And I bet they're pretty big ones too."

Roger took the iron handle and gave it a

tug. Nothing happened at all. He tried again.

"It'll be stiff," said Barney. "It can't have been used for years. Let me try."

He couldn't budge the trapdoor either. Loony went and scraped madly at it as if he could open it that way. They all sat back and panted after their exertions.

"Where's that rope we had?" said Barney, suddenly. "Let me see, what did I do with it? I believe it's upstairs in the nursery, Snubby. Go and get it."

Snubby shot off with Loony, but when he got to the passage door, he heard noises beyond. He stopped, frightened. Who was it? He tore down the stairs again and into the dairy. "There's somebody upstairs. I heard them."

"Don't be silly," said Barney. "You're a little coward, Snubby! There's nobody there."

"There is I tell you – I heard them," said Snubby. Barney got up.

"I'll go," he said, and up he went. He came down with the rope, and with Miranda too. He was grinning.

"It was Miranda up there," he said. "She'd got a box of skittles and was throwing them all over the place. That's what you heard. Baby!"

Snubby went very red. The others laughed at him while Barney slid the rope through the handle of the trapdoor. He twisted the two strands into one.

"Here you are," he said to the other three. "Take hold, all of you, and we'll pull together. Miranda, you pull too!"

So, with Miranda pulling as well, and looking extremely proud, the children pulled together with all their might.

And, of course, the trapdoor opened so very suddenly that they all sat down in a heap, and Roger, who was last, got a terrific bump that shook all the breath out of him!

They got up and went to peer into the dark hole under the trapdoor.

"Steps," said Roger. "Stone steps. They go down to the cellars, no doubt about that. Got the torch, Barney?"

"I'll go first," said Barney, and down he went, flashing the torch carefully in front of him. The steps curved a little towards the bottom and ended in a stone floor. Barney felt it with his feet to see if it was slimy. No, it was quite dry.

A musty smell of old casks and barrels came to his nose. He flashed the torch round. It was, as he had suspected, a most enormous cellar. Boxes, casks, barrels, old cobwebbed bottles lay about everywhere. Wooden shelves showed where wine had once been stored.

Everyone was now down the steps. Miranda would not leave Barney's shoulder,

and held on to his hair as he made his way into the depths of the cellar. The others followed, flashing their torches too. Loony, surprised at this new place so unexpectedly opened in the depths of the earth, ran about sniffing. Any rabbits down here? Not even a smell of one!

The children explored the old cellars from end to end. They opened the old boxes but found nothing in any of them. They knocked on casks and barrels and decided they were absolutely empty. "Not even a full bottle of ginger beer," said Snubby, mournfully. "Very dull."

Mice or rats scurried away into corners as the torches lit them up. Loony had a lovely time chasing them, and got a bite on the ear. Miranda wouldn't chase rats. Loony got a rat in a corner behind a cask, and began to scrape there after it. The cask fell, and three more fell too, making a terrific noise in the old cellars. Everyone jumped.

"It's only Loony," said Roger, relieved. "I say, Barney, I wish we could hear those strange noises now. We should know what part of the cellar they came from."

"I think it's very strange," came Barney's voice from another corner. "There doesn't seem to be anything here to account for those noises at all, and honestly, I can't see any signs of people being here. There's dust in quite a lot of places, but no footprints again, no cigarette ends, nothing!"

"Well, how can we solve the mystery?" demanded Snubby.

"I think I shall come down here one night when I hear the noises and watch," said Barney. "Or better still I could hide myself before the noises begin."

"Would you dare?" said Snubby, in horror. "Gracious, you must be brave."

"Yes, I certainly wouldn't dare to do that," said Diana, soberly. "Would you, Roger?"

Roger thought about it. "No, I don't think I would," he said. "And what's more I don't think you'd better, Barney."

"Well, I'm going to," said Barney. "I can't make all this out. I'm going to find out what's going on."

They sat silently for a few minutes on one or two old boxes while Loony snuffled round them. Barney pricked up his ears. "Can you hear anything?" he asked the others.

They listened. "Well," said Diana doubtfully, "I think I can hear a noise occasionally but I don't quite know how to describe it – rather a gurgly sort of noise."

This didn't please Snubby at all. He got up. He had no wish to hear any noises, least of all "gurgly" ones. Anyway he was tired of this awful dark, musty cellar. He wanted to be out in the daylight again.

"Come on. Don't let's listen for gurgles or gobbles or gluggings," he said.

The others laughed and got up too. Barney listened for a moment or two more and gave it up. "Probably my imagination," he said.

They went up the stone steps, chattering, with Loony bounding in front. At the top he stopped and growled. The children ceased talking at once and Diana clutched at Barney. Now what?

There was the sound of men's voices! "Did we lock that veranda door?" whispered Roger. "Gosh, we didn't! What idiots! Now someone has got in!"

"I'll go and see," whispered Barney. "Keep Loony back and don't let him growl or bark, or he'll give us away."

Snubby put his hand on Loony's collar and the dog stopped his low growling. Barney went quietly through the outhouse and into the scullery. He stopped to listen. Nobody was in the kitchen beyond. He went to the kitchen door and peered through the crack of the door there into the hall.

What he saw surprised him very much! Mr King was there with two other men. Both were strong, burly men, and had their backs to Barney. They were talking together.

"See all these footprints?" Mr King was saying. "That tells you something doesn't it!

We'll have to find out whose they are. And who left the veranda door ajar too? Look at the footmarks going up the stairs. Crowds of them! Looks as if there are troops of people using this place for their own purposes! And yet there's never anyone to be found here when I come, and not a light to be seen anywhere. Where do they go?"

"Beats me," said one of the men. "Anyway, this is the place all right. We'll get going now, no doubt about that."

Barney had heard enough. He slipped back to the others. "It's Mr King with two others," he whispered. "I don't believe they're up to any good here, really. There's some strange plan or something going on, and Mr King's in it. I don't believe he's a tutor at all. He's a fraud!"

This was amazing news. Diana clutched at Barney. "Will they find us down here? What shall we do?"

"We'll get out, shut the trapdoor, and creep out of the kitchen door," said Barney. "We can take the kitchen key, so that we can get in again if we want to. You can bet anything you like that those fellows will search the house now to find out who's made those footprints everywhere, and when they go they will see that every door and window is fastened so that we can't get in again."

"But we'll have the kitchen door key, so

we can if we want to!" said Snubby, who was trembling with excitement. "Is it safe to go now?"

Barney went to see. He came back in half a minute. "They've gone upstairs. I wonder if they know about the nursery. Anyway the passage door is locked and I've got the key. They may think it's only boxrooms or something."

"We'll creep out now, then," said Diana, who was very anxious to go. They all got out of the opening in the floor, and then quietly shut the trapdoor. They made their way into the kitchen, Loony as quiet as the others.

Over to the kitchen door they went and Barney unlocked it. He took the key from the lock and opened the door. It creaked a little but not much. They all went out into an overgrown yard, where an old dustbin still stood. A dog kennel stood nearby, almost falling to bits. Loony went over to it and sniffed in it inquisitively. But there was no dog smell left.

Barney locked the door behind them. He put the key in his pocket. He looked up at the windows. Could any one see them if they made a dash for it now? No. Trees overhung the backyard and screened it from overhead.

"Come on," he said. "We'll run for it now. Keep under bushes and trees and don't show yourselves at all."

They ran from the back door, across the yard and into the bushes. There had once been a kitchen garden on the other side of the yard, but it was so overgrown with weeds that it would have been impossible to know what it was now, if it had not been for the apple trees showing here and there, struggling against the ivy that was slowly choking everything.

The children soon found a part of the grounds they knew and quickly made their way home, astonished and puzzled. Was Mr King really a fraud? Ought they to tell Miss Pepper? What was he doing here? And what had Rockingdown Manor and the peculiar noises to do with everything? It was all very puzzling indeed.

"I think we ought to tell Miss Pepper," said Roger, at last. "We'll sleep on it first and then tell her in the morning."

19

Mr King in Charge

But that night something happened which upset all their plans. A telephone call came for Miss Pepper and after she had answered it she came into the study, looking very upset.

"Children – I have to go away for a few days. My sister is very ill, dangerously ill, and I must go to her. I must leave you in Mr King's charge. You will be quite all right, and I shall put you on your honour to be as good as you can."

"Oh, Miss Pepper, I'm sorry about your sister!" cried Diana. "Is there anything we can do? Are you leaving tonight or tomorrow morning?"

"Tonight, I think. Oh dear, I can't make up my mind what to do. Can I catch the night-train, or not? There is my packing to do, and I must see Mrs Round before I go."

"You can give me any messages for Mrs Round," said Diana. "You know I'll help her all I can. And I can do your packing for you too, if you'll put out the things you want. The boys can ring up for a taxi. You will easily be able to catch the night-train."

"What a kind, good child you are!" said Miss Pepper, almost in tears. "Very well, I'll go tonight. Come up and help me pack while I tell you what I want you to say to Mrs Round."

Roger rang up for a taxi. Diana did the packing and listened to the instructions for Mrs Round. "I'll telephone her tomorrow to tell her how things are getting on," said Miss Pepper. "Did I pack my hairbrush? And a clean blouse? Now what have I done with those shoes?"

"They're in your hands, Miss Pepper," said Diana, taking them from her. "Now, do take things easy. You've plenty of time for your train, and I expect your sister will feel much better as soon as she sees you."

"I must talk to Mr King too," said Miss Pepper. "Thank goodness I can leave him in charge of you. He seems very dependable and responsible."

Diana said nothing to that. Because of what she now suspected about Mr King there didn't seem anything to say except things that would upset Miss Pepper and probably upset her plans too! So she went on packing and made no remark.

Mr King came up to condole with Miss Pepper. He had been out for one of his walks. He was very sweet to her and she felt comforted.

"I feel quite safe to leave the children with you and Mrs Round," she said. "I only hope they'll behave themselves – but I think they will, Mr King. They always come out well in an emergency and are really very trustworthy."

She went off in a taxi, still looking very worried. Everyone waved cheerily to her.

"Well!" said Mr King, shutting the door. "Poor Miss Pepper! I hope everything goes all right for her. Now children, we've got to make the best of one another! You'll have to put up with me being in charge of you!"

He beamed round at them. They looked away. "Er – we shall do our best, Mr King," said Roger, feeling that somebody certainly ought to say something. Mr King looked faintly surprised at the children's lack of response, but put it down to their being upset at Miss Pepper's sudden going.

He looked at his watch. "My word – we *are* all late tonight!" he said. "I think we ought to go to bed. Off with you! Lights out in ten minutes, please."

The three of them had their lights out in ten minutes. They wondered about Barney. He wasn't going to sleep in the old house tonight. They had taken cushions and a rug to the old summerhouse for him, hoping that it would not rain. The summerhouse was not very weatherproof nowadays.

When they were sure that Mr King was in bed they stole down the back stairs to find Barney in the summerhouse, and tell him the news about Miss Pepper's leaving.

"We haven't been able to tell Miss Pepper what we suspect," finished Roger. "That must wait till she comes back. In the meantime we must keep our eyes and ears open!"

"I wonder if I ought to go back and sleep in the old house tonight," said Barney. "Just in case there's something being planned there by Mr King and the other men."

"No, don't," said Roger. "Mr King is indoors now – look, you can see his light through the curtains of his bedroom window. If he has any ideas of wandering over to the mansion again tonight, he will have to pass near the summerhouse, and then you can follow him."

"Yes. There's something in that," said Barney, snuggling down in his rug. "I don't really feel like scrambling through the grounds again at the moment. I feel rather sleepy."

"Well, we'll go back to the cottage now," said the others. "Goodnight, Barney. See you tomorrow."

It seemed strange without Miss Pepper the next day. Mrs Round arrived and heard the news. "Dear, dear, she's so fond of her sister, too," she said. "Well, we must hope for the best. Now you don't need to bother your heads about anything except just do a bit of shopping for me now and again, and make your own beds and give a hand at times."

They all had their tutoring as usual, though Mr King seemed lost in thought. If they hadn't been on their honour to behave themselves they could have played any amount of tricks on the absent-minded tutor. But not even Snubby thought out any. Barney sat as usual in the window, listening. He looked earnestly at the back of Mr King's head and thought about him. What was he doing at Rockingdown Manor? What was he interested in there? It must be something important or he wouldn't have gone to the trouble of taking the job here as tutor – which meant that he could live near the Manor, and find it easier to carry out his plans.

Barney couldn't imagine what those plans were. He wondered if by any chance the three men had done anything in the house after the children had escaped in such a hurry; had they hidden something there, perhaps? Or found something they were looking for?

He slipped out of the room before the end of the lesson.

He felt that he wanted to go and see if anything had been done at the old house; the men certainly hadn't got in for nothing.

He saw nothing at all on the ground floor except for the footmarks of the three men in every room. He took the trouble of going into the outhouses to see if the trapdoor had been discovered.

It was wide open! The wooden trapdoor was swung back, and the flight of stone steps was plainly to be seen.

Barney went to the open trapdoor. He listened. All was quiet now. But obviously the three men had been down to search for something.

He went up to the first floor and saw the prints of the men there, in every room. They had walked to every cupboard. Some of the doors were left open. What could they be looking for? A secret hiding-place?

Up the stairs to the second floor went the boy, feeling certain that the locked door at the end of the passage would have been opened.

It had been burst open! Somebody had either kicked it or flung himself hard against it. The old lock had given way, and the door was swinging wide open.

"Now my hiding-place is discovered!" thought Barney. He went into the nursery. The three beds had been stripped and the covers thrown to the ground. The chests had been looked through, the cupboards opened. Even the linoleum in the day nursery had been taken up.

The rooms were in a dreadful state now. It would need a good morning's work to get them straight again. Barney wondered if it was safe for him to sleep there any more. Well, as long as the good weather lasted he could sleep comfortably in the old summerhouse at Rockingdown Cottage.

It was all very puzzling. Barney made up his mind about one thing straight away. He would certainly go down into the cellars and wait for those noises that night! He meant to get to the bottom of those. Had those three men anything to do with them?

He went back to the children after he had bought himself some bread and cheese at the village shop. He gave Miranda some plums to eat. She liked those. She pulled each plum in half, took out the stone, threw it away, joined the two halves together, and then nibbled the plum in delight.

"You want a bib, Miranda," said Barney, with a laugh. "Those plums are so juicy that you're getting sticky all down your chest!"

After his meal Barney went to see the children. He told them what he had discovered in the old house – the open trapdoor, the footmarks everywhere, the burst-open door, and the rifled nursery. They listened in amazement.

"How dare Mr King do all that!" said Diana. "After I'd made everything so tidy for you too. It's too bad. I've a good mind to tick him off."

"No. Don't you say a word," said Barney, quickly. "Don't put him on his guard at all. As long as he thinks we don't suspect anything wrong about him he won't try to hide his doings. If he guesses what we know, he may go off – and while he is here we have at least got him under our eyes!"

"Yes, that's true," said Diana. "Well, I won't say a word. Barney, I hate the idea of your going to watch down in the cellar tonight. Wouldn't you like one of us with you?"

"Of course not!" said Barney with a laugh. "What do you think could happen to me down there? Nothing, of course!"

But for once Barney was wrong.

20

Down in the Cellars

None of the three children at Rockingdown Cottage felt very friendly towards Mr King, and he was puzzled. Even Loony sat with his back to him whenever he could! The spaniel always knew when Snubby was doubtful about anyone, and if his master would not be friendly towards someone, then Loony behaved in the same way.

Mr King looked at the children three or four times during their midday meal. How odd they were all of a sudden! Anyone would think he had offended them in some way, he thought. They wouldn't look at him, and hardly smiled at all. They hardly spoke to him either.

"Anything the matter?" he said at last. "You seem to be a very gloomy lot today. Are you worried about something?"

"Well – yes," said Diana. "We're worried about Miss Pepper's sister, of course."

"Dear me, I didn't think you even knew her," said Mr King in astonishment. "Well, do cheer up. I'm sure you'll hear things are all right."

Miss Pepper did ring up shortly after that, but the news was not very good. Her sister was still very ill and Miss Pepper didn't know when she would be back. "But I'm sure you'll be all right with Mr King," she said. "And Mrs Round is very good too."

Mr King kept trying to cheer the children up. He offered to take them for a walk. He offered to fix up a riding lesson for them. He even suggested going down to the river to swim as it was a hot day. In the ordinary way the last two suggestions would have been hailed with glee – but nobody felt that they wanted to take any favours from Mr King at the moment. He was a fraud. They weren't going to like him any more. He was up to something, and they wanted to know what!

Mr King gave up his efforts at last, decided that the children were sulky and cross, and they could jolly well look after themselves. Loony annoyed him most. He couldn't believe that a dog would sit with his back to him on purpose, but it really did look as if Loony meant to!

Barney stayed to tea. The children had it out in the garden, hoping to get away from Mr King. But he most annoyingly came and had it with them. He seemed to feel that he must look after them every minute, now

Miss Pepper was away. So the children couldn't talk freely at all, and Diana grew very sulky. She was the worst of them at hiding her feelings.

"You really are a set of miseries!" said Mr King. "Take that sulky look off your face, Diana, it doesn't suit you at all!"

Diana immediately looked twice as sulky. Barney felt that Mr King would really begin to suspect something if they all behaved like this, so he began to talk to the tutor, relating all kinds of tales, and livening things up considerably. Miranda also did her best by behaving very badly with Loony; snatching away a biscuit Diana was giving him, and throwing plum stones at him.

Everyone laughed at her ridiculous antics except Loony, who was very hurt. Mr King felt quite relieved to find that they *could* laugh!

They escaped from the tutor after tea, and went to the village to buy ice creams. The old lady in the general store seemed to keep her shop open till all hours at night and it was possible to get ice creams from dawn to dark at her exciting little shop.

"Don't let's go back to supper till we've got to," said Diana. "I just can't bear Mr King now that I know he's a fraud. Let's go over the grounds and see if we can find that stream."

"Oh yes, that's a good idea," said Roger.

"I've been puzzling my head where it is. It's shown so very close to the old house on the map."

They explored the grounds very thoroughly indeed, north, south, east and west, but there was no sign of a stream at all!

"There's not even a dried-up bed, or a ditch," said Roger, puzzled. "The map must be wrong."

"I suppose it must be," said Barney. "Anyway, as I said, we can always trace where it goes by following its course up from the river. Still – it's not important."

"I don't like to think of you down in those cellars tonight," began Diana again, as they made their way back to the cottage. "I really don't. You'll take your rug and cushion down there with you, won't you? You may as well be comfortable. That floor will be hard and cold."

"Yes. I'll take them," said Barney. "And look, I've bought myself a new torch – grand, isn't it!"

He showed his torch to them. It certainly was a nice one and gave out a very good light. "I shall be all right with this!" he said.

Mrs Round had left enough supper for Barney, so he stayed. He always enjoyed his meals with the children. Afterwards they played a game, while Mr King read.

"I'd better be going," said Barney at last.

Mr King looked up. "Where do you sleep at night?" he asked, and he spoke the words in such a pointed way that the children felt sure he suspected Barney of sleeping up in the nursery of Rockingdown Manor.

"I slept in the summerhouse last night," said Barney, politely. "And last week I slept in the boat with a rug and a cushion. I haven't a proper home, and lodgings are expensive."

"I see," said Mr King. "Well, so long as you don't get into mischief! I suppose you're sleeping in the summerhouse again tonight as it's a hot night – well, look out for a storm, if so."

"Yes, I will," said Barney. His eyes gleamed as he looked at Mr King. What would the tutor say if he knew he was sleeping in the cellars of the old house?

Barney went off with Miranda. The children went with him to the gate, Loony too. He was always glad to see the back of Miranda!

Diana watched Barney out of sight. She was worried. "I do hope he'll be all right," she said.

"Course he will!" said Roger. "Nothing will happen to old Barney. Anyway, he's like a cat – he'll always fall on his feet. He'll look after himself all right."

Barney unlocked the kitchen door of the old house when he got there, and let himself in. He took a quick glance round the ground floor. Nothing had altered since the morning. He went upstairs to get his rug and cushion. The nursery was just the same as when he had seen it this morning – untidy and higgledy-piggledy, drawers and cupboards open everywhere.

Barney picked up his rug and the cushion. He went downstairs with Miranda, yawning. He thought he would get a little sleep straight away, then if the noises began he would be wide awake and fresh.

Miranda was astonished to find that Barney was going to sleep down in the dark cellars. She was not at all pleased at the idea. She chattered angrily and pulled at the rug as if to say "No, no, come upstairs! This is all wrong!"

"Sorry, Miranda, but this is where we sleep tonight!" said Barney, firmly. "Now, where do you think would be a good corner?"

All the corners were equally dirty. In the end Barney thought it would be quite a good idea to lie on one of the wooden shelves that had once held bottles. Wood was not as cold or hard as stone.

He climbed up on a shelf, put the cushion down for his head, and wrapped himself up in the thick rug. The cellars were cold, but it was a very warm night. Barney thought he would be all right in the rug, with Miranda cuddled to him like a hot-water bottle! She snuggled down protestingly.

Barney fell asleep at once, hard though his bed was. A spider ran over his face, but didn't disturb him. When it ran over Miranda's hairy little face she put up a quick paw and caught it. Then she too went to sleep.

Barney slept on peacefully. Half past ten came, eleven o'clock, half past eleven, midnight. Then Barney was awakened by the hardness of his bed. One of his arms was aching through being bent underneath him on the hard board. He shifted his position, remembered where he was, and sat up to listen. Were there any noises at all?

The cellars were very, very quiet and in the silence Barney again thought he caught the faint noise he had heard once before, with Diana. Was it a kind of gurgle? It had gone before he had made up his mind. It was so faint and far-off that it was quite impossible to tell what it was, if it was anything.

He switched his torch on and shone it round. Nothing was to be seen except a pair of frightened rat's eyes gleaming. Then the rat scampered away to a corner and disappeared.

Barney lay down again and Miranda snuggled into his neck, putting her paws inside his shirt for warmth. Barney liked the feel of the tiny monkey-hands. He patted Miranda affectionately, and she nibbled the skin of his neck, also affectionately. She had some funny little ways!

Barney soon fell asleep again. One o'clock came – two o'clock – and then Barney was awakened suddenly.

Thud! Bang!

He shot up straight and Miranda fell off the shelf. The boy listened intently.

BANG!

The noises were very much louder down here. But they couldn't be in the cellars! They sounded too far away for that.

Barney listened hard. When he was sure

that the noises were not in the cellars he switched on his torch. He flashed it all round – no, there was absolutely nothing to be seen. But the noises went on!

Bang! Thud! And then there came the whining noise, and after that a curious grating sound, guttural and harsh. Then Barney felt sure he could hear voices. But they were muffled voices, as if there was a wall or two between them and Barney.

"Well! This is certainly where we do a spot of exploring," said Barney to Miranda, and he threw aside his rug. He jumped down from the wooden shelf and stood listening. He must go in the direction of the noises.

They came from the right. He went in that direction and came up against a stone wall. The noises seemed to be on the other side. But how could they be? There was no way of getting to the other side.

Barney ran his torch along the stone wall on his right. It was just the same as the rest of the cellar walls, except that it was glistening with damp.

Thud! That noise really did sound as if it were behind the wall. Well then, there must be some place behind there! Barney shone his torch again. And then he found what he was looking for! He wouldn't have seen it but for Miranda – it was really she who found it for him.

21

Strange Happenings

An old box stood against the wall. Miranda saw something moving there – was it a spider – a moth? In a second she was after it! She slid down behind the box and Barney moved it out to see what she was after.

And there in the wall he saw an iron handle. It was low down, and very rusty. He had to kneel down to look at it closely.

Why was there an iron handle so low down in the wall? Surely it wasn't meant to be used for anything? Perhaps in the old, far-off days this cellar was used as a dungeon and prisoners had been tied to the iron ring.

Barney looked at it. He set down his torch, put both hands to the ring and tugged it. It was very fast in the wall and would not move. He pushed. No result. He tugged again whilst Miranda sat close by and watched with great interest.

It was quite by accident that he found the secret of the iron handle. He discovered that it turned round and round. So he turned it with a screwing motion – and something happened!

Barney never found out quite what did happen. The screwing round of the handle seemed to work some kind of lever and suddenly the stone next to the one in which the iron ring was set began to move, very, very slowly! It moved inwards, towards Barney, grating a little as it ran over hidden grooves. He stopped twisting the handle in surprise, and the stone stopped moving. It was half in, half out of the thick wall. Shaking with excitement Barney twisted the iron handle again and once more the stone next to it began to move.

It came right out from its place, leaving a small gap between itself and the wall. Barney looked at the gap. It would take him easily, or a small man. A big man would have difficulty squeezing through. He flashed his torch to the gap, but it was impossible to see what lay behind it.

"Shall we get through?" he said to Miranda. She did not wait to answer, but slipped neatly through herself! She came back at once, chattering.

She was not frightened, so Barney decided there couldn't be much behind the sliding stone. He would go and see. The noises might have their origin behind it somewhere.

So he squeezed through the gap. On the

other side of the wall was pitch darkness! Barney shone his torch round to see what was what.

He was in a very curious place indeed. It was very small, not much bigger than a boxroom, and the ceiling or roof was so low that Barney could not stand upright. The walls were running with damp, and there was a very damp smell there too.

Barney looked round this strange little place in surprise. What in the world was it? There was nothing there at all, as far as he could see.

And then he heard one of the noises. It was so loud that he almost jumped out of his skin! It sounded almost in the little room, but not quite.

It seemed to come from under the ground. Barney flashed his torch on the floor, and how he stared!

Not far from him was a dark hole, quite round and very narrow. It went down for some way because his torch could not pick out the bottom of it. He could see the remains of an old iron ladder going down this curious shaft, and it was up this hole that the noises came!

They sounded very loud indeed when he stood at the top of the hole. Miranda was terrified. She bounded back to the gap in the wall and shot through it, gibbering with fright. Barney called her back, but it was a long time before she would come. He had to go to the gap and coax her gently.

She came through again at last, and then something really dreadful happened! Barney must have touched some hidden lever, or pressed some spring, because the stone that had moved out to make the gap began slowly to move back again. At first Barney did not realise what was happening. He was fondling Miranda and trying to make her less frightened.

Then a small noise made him look up and to his horror he saw that the gap was almost closed! He tried to catch hold of the moving stone and push it out again but it was heavy and he couldn't stop it going right back into its place.

Barney got into a panic then. He was cold and damp in that horrid little space with its streaming walls. He hunted frantically for any iron ring or lever that would set the stone moving again, so that he might squeeze through the gap. He was a prisoner if he couldn't find it! There must be some way of getting the stone to move from this side – or wasn't there? Surely this could not be a horrible little dungeon where unwanted prisoners were hidden long ago?

Another noise boomed up through the strange hole. Warm now with his exertions at trying to find some way of moving the stone out again, Barney stopped to listen.

If men were causing that noise, then there must be a way of escape down that hole! But where in the world did it lead to? Barney didn't want to go down at all. It was so black and narrow and the iron ladder was not safe.

He made some more frantic efforts to find a way to move the stone, but it was no use. It couldn't be done. He walked the three steps to the hole and looked down it. Again he thought he heard voices. Were they really voices? If there were men down there they might help him, except that whatever they were doing must be very secret, and probably against the law. They would certainly not be pleased to see him!

Supposing Mr King was down there too! That would be a funny state of affairs! Well – not funny. Things were far from funny at the moment, in fact they were horribly serious.

There was nothing for it but to begin climbing down that fearsome shaft. Barney knelt on the stone floor and gingerly put one leg down into the hole. His foot felt about for the ladder. He found a bar and let his weight go down on it.

It broke at once! Well, this was going to be very difficult indeed if the ladder wasn't going to hold him!

He felt for the next rung. His weight pressed down on it, and that broke too!

Barney began to feel panic-stricken again. Miranda chattered in fright, clinging on his shoulder.

Then Barney felt for the sides of the rungs. Were there staples there, or nails, or even bits of broken rung?

He found a sharp piece of iron, the bit of rung that was driven into the wall of the shaft. He decided that it would be best to tread on the ends of the rungs, because then possibly they would not break. They would certainly break if he trod in the middle of them. So, very carefully indeed Barney felt about for another rung and trod gingerly at the very edge of it, where it was driven into the shaft wall. Each one held now and Barney breathed more easily.

Soon his whole body was in the hole, his feet feeling for the edges of the rungs, his hands holding on to the ones above his head. Down he went and down. Where did the hole lead to? One of the noises came up as he descended and Miranda nearly fell off his shoulder in fright.

The hole was about four metres deep. It came to an end at last. Barney felt his feet on solid ground. He let go and turned himself round. There was a kind of doorway in the shaft wall behind him, low and narrow. Barney stooped and went through it.

Now he could plainly hear the voices of men, shouting and calling to one another.

Then he jumped. He heard that screeching, whining sound. He guessed what it was now. It was some machine – a winch, perhaps, being worked.

He squinted round, not yet daring to put on his torch again. He had switched it off as soon as he found his feet on solid ground. He stood there in the dark, listening, not wanting to take a step forward or backwards in case he fell down yet another hole!

Then he became conscious of another sound, a sound that went on and on all the time – a quiet sound that occasionally became louder. The sound of water!

"Yes, that's it, it's water!" said Barney to himself in amazement. "Where is it? It sounds awfully near." He switched his torch on and off quickly for a moment. He was in a narrow passage that slanted down from the shaft-hole. At the end of the passage was the gleam of water!

"Well!" said Barney, in amazement. "What is it? An underground pool?"

He walked cautiously down the narrow passage and came to the water, shading his torch with his hand so that its light would not easily be seen. Yes, there was the water, black and gleaming, and flowing along!

Flowing along! Then it must be a river of some kind; no, not a river, a stream, because it wasn't wide enough for a river.

And then, in a flash Barney knew what it was! It was Rockingdown Stream – the stream shown on the map as flowing near, very near, Rockingdown Manor! Not only did it flow near, but it must flow practically under the old house! No wonder the wall near the shaft-hole was damp.

Forgetting to be cautious he flashed his torch on the stream. It flowed in a rocky bed, and there was an arched rocky roof to it, that was very low in places. Beside it, on the side that Barney stood, was a ledge, wide enough to walk on. There was no ledge at all on the other side.

What an extraordinary thing! A river flowing under the house, and men working by it in the tunnel, making weird noises underground that sounded up in the old house – muffled and distant, but still easy to hear!

Barney wondered if the men knew that their noises could be heard. Still, even if they knew, they wouldn't care, because they thought the old house was completely deserted – there would be no one there to hear!

From some way down to the left, the way the stream was flowing, a dim light showed. It was from there the sound of voices and other noises came. Barney made his way carefully along the rocky ledge beside the stream, crouching where the roof swept down low. He came out on the other side of the low roof, and saw that the stream curved round to the left. Round the corner the light was brighter – that was evidently where the men where.

Barney began to feel more cheerful. If men knew a way in to this place, then there was a way out! And he would be able to find it and escape. But before he did that he was going to see what was happening down here!

He came to the place where the river curved to the left, and peeped cautiously round the corner. He was astounded at what he saw. The narrow tunnel in which the stream ran suddenly widened out into a great low-roofed cave, and here the men were at work with a winch, which was making the whining, screeching noise that Barney had so often heard. Another winch was at work nearby, and that had a harsh, guttural sound which was magnified very much in the tunnel.

Barney could make out three men. They were shouting above the noise of the winches. Whatever were they doing? If only he could find out!

22

Any Way of Escape?

Barney stood hidden by a rock that jutted out from the tunnel and watched in astonishment all that was going on. The stream flowed quickly past him, gurgled along at one side of the big low cave, and disappeared again into another tunnel, leaving the cave behind.

Men were working at a couple of winches, which made loud, harsh noises as the rope was wound up on each winch. One of the men gave a shout: "Lights up!"

A bright, glaring lamp was switched on near the stream. Another man appeared from the far tunnel with what looked like a pitchfork in his hand. The winches went on winding. Then a large object appeared, coming out from the far tunnel, bobbing about on the swift-flowing stream, whose current was against it.

Barney stared, his mouth open in surprise. The men were winding in big crates from the far tunnel where the stream disappeared on its swift course. Barney could not make out quite what these crate-like objects were

– great boxes of something? Cases of some-thing heavy? It was impossible to see.

The four men rushed to the crate and it was dragged right into the cave. *Bang! Thud!* It was shifted into place.

Barney craned round as far as he dared to see where the crate was being put. He thought he could see other cases piled together. This must be a hiding place – or sorting place? It was obviously some very secret spot, used for very secret things.

The winches wound again and another crate came bobbing up the tunnel – and yet another. Barney guessed that they must all be tied together in some way. There must be a long line of them down the far tunnel! The man who held what looked like a pitch-fork disappeared into the tunnel, each time a new crate appeared, guiding it deftly as it bobbed along. Barney guessed there was a narrow little rocky ledge by the side of the river just there, just as there had been in his part of the underground tunnel.

"That's the lot!" shouted the man with the pitchfork, as the last crate was man-handled into place. "Now let's clear off! I'm dead!"

Barney crouched back against the rocky side of the tunnel, hoping the men would not come near him. They didn't. They walked off the other way, clambering along the rocky ledge of the distant tunnel and disappearing in the dark, their torches shining out for a time and then vanishing.

The whole place was now in pitch darkness. Miranda, on Barney's shoulder, chattered into his ear. She was cold and tired. She didn't understand this curious adventure at all.

Barney switched on his own torch again, glad he had such a powerful one. He made his way to the low-roofed cave. It was even bigger than he had imagined! It was, in fact, a vast underground cavern, its wall gleaming with phosphorescence here and there.

Piled against one wall were crates of all kinds and sizes. There were names on them that Barney did not understand – were they names of places or people? He didn't know.

He wandered round the big cavern. Right at the end he found what was evidently a kind of workshop or sorting place. Here were empty crates that had been unpacked. There was nothing to show what had been in them except for a stack of dull, leaden-looking bars. Barney picked one up. It was very heavy. He thought it might be a bar of silver – silver that had been melted down.

"Perhaps stolen silver articles are melted down into these bars," thought the boy. "Perhaps this is a kind of central receiving place for stolen or smuggled goods – what a wonderful hiding place! Nobody would ever guess where it was!"

He wandered all round the big cavern. He found something that pleased him very much, an old mattress with rugs and a pillow, and, even better, a ledge on which were stacked tins of meat and fruit!

The men evidently had meals down here sometimes in the middle of a big job and maybe even slept here on occasion. Well, Barney would sleep here too, if he had to, and have a meal as well! If he couldn't find a way of escape at once, he could make himself comfortable till he did find one. In the meantime he would find out all he could.

He looked at the winches. They were powerful ones. They needed to be to drag those crates against the fast-flowing water, and how far did they have to be dragged? Barney began to wonder about that too.

He decided not to explore any more for the present. He was tired and cold and he had had enough adventures for the time being. He would lie down on the mattress and sleep. Miranda would wake him if she heard anyone coming.

He lay down and was soon asleep, Miranda cuddled up to him once more. He did not know how long he slept for he had no watch, and, as it was always dark in the underground cavern, he could not tell, on waking, if it was daytime or not.

But he felt as if it must be, when he awoke. He was hungry so he went to the collection of tins. Ah! – tins of ham. He would open one of those – if there was an opener! He saw a pile of tin plates and dishes nearby, with a little heap of cheap knives, forks and spoons. With them were two tin-openers.

Barney was soon enjoying a meal of tinned ham, and peaches from another tin. He hid the empty tins behind a rock so that if the men came back they wouldn't suspect anything.

He felt a good deal better after that, in fact he felt fit for anything! Miranda, who had gobbled up four half-peaches in delight, was also ready for anything. She bounded round the cave, examining this and that, and then, quite suddenly, the place was flooded with a dazzling light.

Barney leaped to his feet, blinking, expecting to see the men returning. But nobody appeared. Then how did the light come on so suddenly?

He laughed, of course, it was that monkey Miranda. She had come across the light switch and turned it on, flooding the cave with light! She loved meddling about with any switches she found, and had often got herself into trouble over this. He called to her.

"Naughty Miranda! Don't meddle! Turn it off again."

Miranda made a chattering noise, full of glee. She switched the light on and off several times. Finally she switched it off and left the place in darkness again, except for Barney's torch.

"Come here, Miranda," called Barney. "It's time we got out of here. We're going down the river. If the men have a way of escape there, so have we!"

Miranda leaped to his shoulder and held

on to his right ear. Barney went to where the stream disappeared into the far tunnel, and flashed his torch down it. Beside the water ran a very narrow ledge of rock, much narrower than the ledge he had scrambled down before. Also, at times it was not above the level of the stream, but below, which meant wading through the cold water for some way.

The tunnel did not run straight, but curved about, and the stream curved with it. It was a weird journey, walking beside the black water, on a terribly narrow ledge of rock. At one place the tunnel roof was so low that Barney was forced to go on his hands and knees, and Miranda screamed in terror. She didn't like water.

After about ten minutes of this Barney was quite fed up. But he had to go on. On he went for another fifteen minutes and then he saw a dim light in front of him. What was it? He hurried along as fast as he could, hoping it was daylight.

He came to a great iron gate! Beyond the gate was daylight, obscured by enormous strands of greenery that hung down over the bars! This was where the stream flowed out from the underground into the open. Barney stopped and stared at the iron gate. It was very old, very stout, very overgrown. It could never have been meant to open. It had been built from the low roof of the tunnel right down to the bed of the stream, allowing the water to flow out between the bars.

Barney did not even try to shake the gate or move it in any way. It was quite plain that nobody had gone out that way – nobody could! It must have been built years ago, to stop people exploring up the underground stream, so curiously flowing out of the hill on which the old house stood.

The boy stood looking through the thick curtain of greenery that dimmed the daylight. Brambles, ferns, and creeping plants climbed across the iron gate. It was impossible to get out of this strange prison behind the bars! "The men can't have escaped through this," thought Barney. "Well, where did they go, then? I must have missed their way of exit. I'll go back."

So back he went, stumbling along the rocky ledge again, looking carefully everywhere to see if he had missed the men's way of departure from the tunnel. And then Miranda suddenly gave one of her little excited chatterings. She had seen something! It was about halfway up the tunnel. Barney flashed his torch all around but at first could see nothing but the rocky sides of the river tunnel, and the narrow ledge he was standing on.

Then Miranda suddenly left his shoulder and swung herself over the water. She grasped something in mid-air and rocked to and fro! Barney flashed his torch on her. She was swinging on a rope!

"Gosh! A rope! Where does it come from?" said Barney in astonishment. His torch picked out the thick, sturdy rope. It ran up to the roof of the tunnel, and there, in the roof, was what looked like flat pieces of board. Barney stared, puzzled. A rope hanging down from boarding in the roof of the tunnel.

He worked it out. There must be a hole in the roof of the tunnel there – either a natural one, or man-made. It was possible that there was a dip in the ground above and that the surface was quite near the tunnel roof. A hole had been found – or made – the river below discovered and explored and the cavern found.

"The men must have used this as their way of escape," thought Barney. "Once the boards are taken up, and they climb through the hole, they are above ground. I wonder if this is the place where the crates are brought, and lowered down into the water. It must be."

He swarmed up the rope, hanging above the water. But he could not move the boards lying in place across the hole in the roof. Something heavy must have been put on top of them, to hide them. He dropped down, disappointed.

He worked out what the men did. "They

bring the crates and boxes here at night, they remove the boards that hide the hole in the tunnel roof. They drop the goods down into the water and fasten them to a wire rope that runs up the stream to those winches. Then, it's just a question of dragging them up the water, guiding them as they go! What a very ingenious idea – nobody in the world would guess such a hiding-place!"

But working out the ingenious idea didn't help Barney to escape! There he was, a prisoner underground, and with no way out at all!

23

Where Can Barney Be?

Next day the children wondered what in the world had happened to Barney. He didn't appear for breakfast, though he had said he would. He didn't even appear when the time came for lessons, and that was very disturbing. Barney never missed his morning's listening!

"Where is he?" wondered Roger. "I hope he's all right."

Diana was very worried indeed. When Barney didn't appear at lunch-time she was quite beside herself. "I know something's happened to him!" she said. "We must all go and look for him in the old house. We'll go down to the cellars and see if we can find out anything there."

Mr King couldn't make the children out at all. They obviously had some worry, but they wouldn't tell him a thing, and when he came near they stopped talking at once.

"I must say I think your behaviour is peculiar," he remarked to Diana. "Why don't you tell me what's wrong? I might be able to do something. Where's Barney?"

"He'll probably turn up," said Roger at once. Certainly they were not going to tell Mr King their worries. As for peculiar behaviour – well, what about his?

So they told him nothing, and he felt very cross. Miss Pepper phoned to say that her sister was better. Perhaps it would not be very long before she could come back. Mr King was relieved. Maybe the children would behave in a more normal way when Miss Pepper was back.

After lunch they set off for the old house. Loony was very pleased to be out. He didn't like it when the children stayed in the house and went into huddles over something, and talked earnestly and worriedly, never noticing him at all.

First of all the three went up to the nursery with Loony. They had wondered at first how to get in, but had found that Barney had not locked the kitchen door; whether purposely or not, they didn't know. The untidy, dishevelled nursery shocked Diana. How dare Mr King mess it up like this.

"Don't bother about putting it straight now, Di," said Roger. "We'd better go over all the house and down into the cellars straight away, just in case Barney's ill or hurt, and wants help. You never know. It's so strange that he hasn't turned up today."

They went all over the house. Nothing to be seen. Then they went down to the kitchen, through the scullery and into the outhouses. The trapdoor in the dairy was wide open.

"Well – down we go," said Roger, switching on his torch, and down they went, carefully descending the steep stone steps. Now they were in the dark cellars. They called Barney.

"Barney! Where are you? Are you here?"

Echoes answered them eerily. "Here! Here! Here!"

"He's not here," said Roger. "Loony, go and look for him."

Loony was soon sniffing into every corner. It was he who found the wooden shelf on which Barney had slept the night before. He stood by it and barked loudly. They saw the rug and the cushion on the shelf at once.

"There! That's where he slept last night!" said Roger. "But where is he now? And where's Miranda?"

The children sat down on a box to think what to do next.

While they were sitting there Loony ran sniffing round the cellars, trying to smell where Barney had been. He came to the corner where the iron ring was, low in the wall. He scraped at it, whining, smelling Barney's smell there.

Snubby ran over to him. "What is it,

Loony? What have you found? I say, you others, what do you think this is?"

They all knelt in the corner and examined the iron ring set in the wall. Just as Barney had done they pushed and pulled. But unfortunately nobody thought of turning it round and round, so they did not discover the secret of the moving stone. They gave it up after a time.

"It's nothing," said Roger. "It's not worth bothering about. I expect Loony's only excited because he can smell rats there or something."

So they left the iron ring and went up the steps into the dairy. It was nice to be in the daylight again.

"Well, Barney's not here," said Snubby, dolefully. "Let's go. This house gives me the creeps today. It really does."

"What shall we do about Barney?" said Diana to Roger. "Do you think we ought to report that he's disappeared?"

"Not yet," said Roger. "We'd feel awfully silly if we did that and then Barney walked in with Miranda, grinning all over his face as usual!"

"All right," said Diana. "We won't then. But if he doesn't turn up tomorrow I really think we ought to tell somebody. I wish Miss Pepper was at home. We can't possibly tell Mr King. And we don't know anyone else here."

They went soberly out of the kitchen door and pulled it to. They began to make their way through the grounds.

"What shall we do for the rest of the afternoon?" said Roger.

"Well, we won't go riding or swimming," said Diana. "Just in case Barney comes in to tea. I want to be about when he does come, in case he's got any news for us."

"I know," said Snubby, suddenly. "We could take the short cut to that stream I saw the other day when I was tracking Mr King, and we could follow it up and see where it goes to. We could find out where the map goes wrong."

"It's not a very exciting thing to do but we may as well do it," said Roger. "Come on, Loony, leave that rabbit-hole alone. You'll never get down it. You're too fat!"

Off they went with Loony at their heels. They went to Rockingdown Cottage for the map, and discovered that Mr King had gone out, Mrs Round told them.

"He went off over that way, with his stick," she said, pointing down the hill. "He said he'd be back for tea."

"Blast! That's the way we want to go," said Roger, looking at the map. "See, we take this path and then go down there, round that little wood, then on down the hill till we come to the stream. This spot must be about where Snubby saw the hidden boat. We'll make for that and then follow the stream upwards and see where it goes."

They set off with Loony, who was very pleased at the prospect of a second walk. Perhaps he would find rabbit-holes big enough to get down this time! That was always Loony's biggest hope.

It didn't take them long to find the stream. "Where's the place where the boat was hidden, Snubby?" said Roger, standing beside the stream that flowed swiftly by.

"See that bunch of willows over there? That looks like the place," said Snubby. They went on again over the marshy fields, Loony cleverly leaping from tuft to tuft of wiry grass; the children, less clever, walked into sodden ground from which they had to pull their feet with a *plop-plop-plop*.

"I don't like this much," said Diana. She stopped and surveyed the big flat field. "It's rather a desolate sort of place – there are trees only where the stream runs. You can easily see its course by the willows and alders on its banks."

"Look, this is the place where the boat was hidden," said Snubby, when they came near to the clump of willows he had pointed out. But the boat was not there! The little backwater was empty.

"Now where's the boat gone?" wondered Snubby.

"Oh well, I suppose whoever owns it has gone for a row!" said Diana.

"But who owns it?" demanded Snubby. "Look all round you; there isn't a single house or cottage in sight!"

There wasn't. What Snubby said was perfectly true. It was really very odd to think of a boat in a little hidden creek and nobody within miles to own it. Anyway the boat was gone now. It wasn't any good puzzling about it.

"Let's follow the stream upwards now," said Roger. "Come on, Loony. This way. Get him, Snubby, he'll fall into the water. He's seen a vole or something."

Snubby rescued Loony from a watery bed and propelled him in front of him. Loony promptly rolled over on his back.

"Right," said Snubby. "If you want to spend the afternoon like that, do! Goodbye!"

Loony soon followed, forgetting his vole. The four of them went along the banks of the stream. It flowed downhill and the current was quite swift. The little stream twisted and curved about as all streams do, making the children walk twice as far as they need have done.

They followed it for about fifteen minutes, and then a steeper hill towered in front of them. "If the stream flows down that it will come pretty fast," said Roger. But it

didn't flow down the hill. It suddenly disappeared behind a curtain of greenery. In fact, it went underground.

"Gosh – it's gone to ground!" said Roger. "Well, that explains the map then, when it showed the stream so near the old house. It must flow almost underneath it, under the ground."

"Yes, of course," said Diana, quite excited. "That's what the explanation is; it's an underground stream as far as here and then it pops out and flows across the marshy fields."

They clambered to where the stream came out from the hill. They could not see the iron gate shutting off the opening of the tunnel because of the thick curtains of brambles and ivy. But Roger, thrusting his hand through the ivy, felt the iron bars.

"There's something here," he said, and began to tear away the ivy strands. "Yes, a gate or barrier of some sort. To stop people going up the stream, I suppose. Perhaps it's dangerous."

"Oh, what a pity! I'd have loved to go up the stream underground and see where it goes," said Snubby. "What a pity Barney isn't here. He would have loved this."

Not many hours before, Barney himself had stood only a metre or two from where they were, but on the other side of the barrier! They didn't know that. They peered through the thick green curtain but could see nothing but darkness there.

"Well, we've solved that mystery," said Roger, climbing down from where he had clung to see through the ivy sprays. "We'd better go back."

"Look! Is that a little backwater there?" said Diana, pointing to the other side of the stream a little way down from the iron gate. "Let's see if it is."

"Well, we really ought to go home," said Roger, looking at his watch. "Still, we'll just see if there's anything interesting there. We might even find the mysterious boat."

They did! They followed the little backwater between a row of alder trees. It curved round very suddenly and entered a dip in the ground where it opened out into a pond. Ducks were on the pond and the boat was there, tied to a tree! Snubby was sure it was the same boat because it had no name!

In a hollow was a farmhouse. Barns rose around it, mellow and with moss on the tiles. It was a lovely place.

"Well – what a surprise!" said Diana. "A farmhouse up here, lost to the world! That's where the boat belongs. No mystery about it at all!"

They went towards the farmhouse. A man came out from a barn and saw them. He looked extremely disagreeable.

"You clear off!" he shouted. "Do you hear? We don't allow hikers here. Be off at once, or I'll set the dogs on you."

Three or four dogs now set up a terrific barking and Loony barked back. But he did not venture any nearer. He was afraid of so many dogs at once!

"All right!" called Roger indignantly. "We're going! Don't worry."

He and the others made their way back down the backwater to the stream and there they had another surprise.

Mr King was there, gazing earnestly at the iron gate, the barrier covered with green!

24

A Very Great Surprise

Mr King was just as surprised to see the three children and Loony as they were to see him. Loony was so astonished that he quite forgot the feud that seemed to lie between Mr King and the children, and hurled himself at him to greet him.

"Well!" said Mr King, in surprise. "Who would have thought of meeting you here!"

"Yes. Odd isn't it?" said Roger politely. Now what was Mr King up to? Had he followed them? What was he doing snooping round in that part of the world again – staring at the iron gate covered with greenery as if he knew some secret about it! Perhaps he knew where Barney was!

"Well, we might as well walk home together," said Mr King, looking at his watch. "We shall be a little late for tea, but I don't expect Mrs Round will mind."

The children didn't want to walk home with him but there was nothing left for it but to agree. So off they all went, Loony rather subdued. He had suddenly remembered that Snubby was not friendly towards Mr King, and he wished he hadn't given him such a welcome!

"Isn't Barney with you?" said Mr King, sounding surprised. "Where's he got to today? Don't you know?"

"Oh, he's got all sorts of things to do," said Roger. "He's about somewhere, I expect. Haven't you seen him, Mr King?"

"You haven't quarrelled, I hope?" said the tutor. This was too silly a suggestion to be answered. Snubby made a noise that sounded rather like "pooh". It would be difficult to quarrel with the good-tempered Barney.

Barney was not waiting for them at teatime. Mrs Round said he hadn't called at all. They ate their tea with Mr King, and began to be really worried again about Barney. What could have happened to him?

"We'll wait till tomorrow morning and then we'll go to the police," said Roger, desperately, when bedtime came and still Barney had not appeared. Diana was almost beside herself with worry. She was very fond of Barney. But Snubby looked the most miserable of them all.

That night Roger woke up with a jump. He had heard something. He sat up and thought for a minute. What had the sound been like? Could it have been made by

Barney? What did it sound like? Yes – it sounded like someone closing the front door very, very softly!

Roger was up in an instant. Without putting on slippers or dressing-gown he went quietly down the stairs. He ran out of the front door, leaving it open. He saw a figure moving down by the gate. There was a little moon that night, and Roger could make out who it was – Mr King!

Yes, Mr King on another of his mysterious night prowls. All right, Roger would follow him and see where he went – he might even lead him to Barney. Roger felt that Mr King was villain enough to keep him prisoner somewhere, for some secret reason of his own!

It was not nice walking in bare feet, especially as Mr King went through the grounds of the old house. He must be going there. Carefully and painfully Roger followed him, biting his lip as he trod on a thorn or stone with his bare feet.

Mr King stopped. Two men materialised out of the bushes. They began to talk in low voices. Roger strained to listen but could only catch a few sentences.

"We got him all right but he won't talk." Then there was some conversation Roger couldn't catch.

"Oh yes, it makes a very good cover! I'll say it does – nobody would ever guess that." More low talk, and then a sentence from Mr King again. "Well, if those kids I tutor guessed what I'm really up to, they'd pass out!"

Roger froze into the bushes. Had they got hold of Barney then? What cover were they talking about – the old house? "All right, Mr King, you think we don't know anything, but we know you're a bad lot all right!" thought Roger, grimly.

The men talked a little while longer and then walked towards the old house. Roger had heard enough. He would go to the police tomorrow and tell them all he knew, and beg them to find Barney. He'd tell them to arrest Mr King too, the fraud! He didn't want to follow the men any farther. His feet were sore and bleeding. He must go back. Anyway he knew enough now to stop Mr King's little game, whatever it was!

He went home to bed, but not to sleep. He puzzled things over in his mind, trying to make out what Mr King was doing, why he had captured Barney, and hundreds of other things that gradually slipped into dreams, and gave him nightmares. He awoke in the morning, anxious and exhausted with his worried sleep.

He told the others what he planned to do. "I'm off to the police," he said. "You sit down and begin lessons as usual with Mr King, so that he doesn't suspect anything.

Just say I've gone to do some urgent shopping for Mrs Round. I know she wants some potatoes. I'll tell her I'll go and get those!"

So Snubby and Diana sat down alone with Mr King. No Barney, no Roger. Diana was pale and looked worried. Mr King looked at her and at the restless Snubby. What on earth was the matter with these three kids ever since Miss Pepper went away?

At about eleven o'clock footsteps came up to the front door – two pairs of footsteps! Diana began to tremble. Had Roger brought back a policeman? She couldn't see who it was from the study window.

The door opened and in came Roger, looking extremely important. Behind him came a burly policeman. Diana gave a gasp. Mr King looked amazed.

"What's all this?" he said, in astonishment. "Roger – you haven't got into trouble, have you?"

"*I* haven't," said Roger.

"It's like this, sir," said the policeman, taking out a notebook and flicking over the pages. "This boy here came and made a report to me, sir, this morning. Seems as if a friend of his has been missing for two days – name of Barnabas, surname not known. And Roger here seems to think you know something about his disappearance."

"This is absurd," said Mr King angrily. "Roger, what do you mean by it?"

"Well, we know all about your night prowlings and your mysterious walks, and your explorations of the old house," said Roger boldly. "You went into Rockingdown Manor and looked everywhere – you messed up the nursery and threw everything all over the place. You meet with strange men at night; you're plotting something with them.

We don't know what it is but we're sure you've got something to do with Barney's disappearance – so I went to the police this morning and reported everything."

"That's right, sir," said the policeman, stolidly. "It's a strange story, sir, and I'd like some kind of explanation, if you please – most particularly about this breaking into Rockingdown Manor. Serious business that, sir."

Mr King was frowning. He glared at Roger, who looked him straight in the face. "Aha!" said Roger's look, "what have you to say to all this, fraud of a Mr King!"

Mr King stood up. He looked rather taller and more imposing all of a sudden. He spoke in a crisp, commanding voice.

"Constable, take a look at this, will you?"

He held something in his hand. The constable took a look and his face slowly went red. He shut up his notebook and backed away hurriedly.

"I beg you pardon, sir. I'd no idea, sir, none at all. I never got any notification from headquarters, sir."

"That's all right," said Mr King, still in his new, crisp voice. "It was thought better to say nothing locally. You can go. I'll deal with this matter now."

The constable went. Even the back of his neck was red, Diana noticed. She was completely overcome with amazement. As for Roger and Snubby, they couldn't make head or tail of anything. They stared at Mr King, bewildered. He sat down again.

"Sit down," he said, and Roger sat. Nobody said a word. Mr King looked round grimly at the three.

"So you were spying on me, were you? What for, I should like to know? And why not come to me straight away and tell me everything, instead of going to a village policeman? Exactly what do you know?"

Nobody answered at first. They felt completely in the dark.

"Mr King – what did you show to the constable, please?" said Diana, at last.

"I showed him something that told him I was somebody considerably higher up in the police force than he was," said Mr King, after a pause. "I'm here on an important investigation. I'm sorry you thought I was the villain of the piece. I assure you I'm not."

There was another silence. Roger felt more foolish and more embarrassed than he had ever felt in his life before. What was Mr King then; a detective, a secret agent, or what? Roger didn't even dare to ask him!

"I'm very sorry, sir," he said at last. "It – it was only because I was so worried about Barney disappearing that I went to the police – and – and – well – told them what

I suspected about you. I'm very sorry."

"I should think so," said Mr King. "But what is all this about Barney disappearing? I didn't know you were really worried about him. Look here – you've been snooping about just as much as I have, evidently, and maybe you know things I don't. We'd better pool our knowledge and help one another instead of working against each other – though I'm blessed if I knew anything about your secret activities at all! Little criminals, the lot of you!"

He smiled, and the children's hearts lightened. He had a nice smile. How could they have thought he was a fraud, a villain? He was somebody important, somebody intensely interesting, somebody unexpectedly commanding and altogether admirable.

"We've been idiots," said Snubby, finding his voice suddenly. "Absolute super-idiots."

"Smashing ones," agreed Mr King, with a wider smile. "I've been a bit of a fraud though, I must confess. I'm not really a tutor! I know enough to teach three ignoramuses like you, though it's not a job I like. I took it because I needed to be somewhere in this neighbourhood, as you have probably guessed by now."

"Yes, we did guess you were a – fraud in that way," Diana agreed, blushing. "Shall we tell you all we know, Mr King? Then perhaps you can help us with Barney."

The three of them told everything. Mr King listened intently. "Well, there's not much I don't know in all you tell me," he said. "Still, it all helps. Now, I'll tell you something, and you'll please keep your mouths shut about it."

The three of them listened, thrilled.

"There's smuggling going on in this neighbourhood," said Mr King. "It's been suspected for a long time. There's a mysterious aeroplane that lands somewhere at night and takes off almost immediately. There's a motor-launch, also mysterious, that appears at times in this neighbourhood, on the river. We think there's a kind of receiving headquarters here – where the stuff is hidden till it's safe to dispose of it or where it is sorted out into small bits for sale and disposed of immediately, somewhere, somehow. But where this hiding-place is, and who are the chief men concerned we don't know. We've got one of the smaller men, but he won't talk. We had an idea that the old house, Rockingdown Manor, was the centre – but we've gone through it with a fine-tooth comb and there's nothing to show that it is. Nothing at all."

"What about those noises?" said Roger, in excitement. "The ones Barney was going to find out about?"

"Ah, those are very, very interesting," said Mr King. "And I think young Barney's disappearance is due to his curiosity about those noises! He's paying for his inquisitiveness, I fear."

"Oh dear," said Diana, going pale. "What – what do you think has happened to him? Where is he?"

"I've no idea," said Mr King. "But we'll find him as soon as we can. There are such a lot of loose ends about all this – that Rockingdown Stream, which runs underground, might lead us to the heart of the mystery, but no, it's blocked up with a completely impassable barrier – so we have to rule that out!"

"It's a good thing Miss Pepper is away," said Snubby suddenly. "She'd have a blue fit about all this."

"Yes – she'd certainly go up in smoke," agreed Mr King. "Now, will you leave me alone for a bit. I must think, and I must remake my plans. I'll see you at lunch-time, and tell you what I'm going to do. So long till then – and cheer up, do, for goodness sake!"

25

Everything is Very Difficult

At lunch-time Mr King told the children his plans.

"I'm pretty certain Barney's disappearance is the result of his poking his nose into this smuggling affair," he said. "We'll have to find him, or things will be serious for him. These men are rogues – real bad fellows who stick at nothing."

Diana was frightened. She stared at Mr King with wide, scared eyes. "What are you going to do, then?" she asked.

"First of all go through Rockingdown Manor again, top to bottom – especially the bottom, where the cellars are," said Mr King. "I feel you're right when you say those strange noises have something to do with all this. Barney must have stumbled on the cause, and now he's disappeared because of it. Though I must say it beats me how the noises are made, and where they come from. If they don't come from the cellars, where can they come from?"

Mr King went on explaining his plans. "I must also find out who that boat belongs to, and have a look at the farmhouse you told me about, and I must examine that gate or barrier thoroughly. It certainly looks as if nobody has moved it for centuries – but we must see. And if *we* can't get up past the barrier, well I'm pretty certain nobody else has been able to push by it!"

"We'll come and help," said Roger eagerly. He looked hard at Mr King. It was puzzling to think how he and the others had been so certain he was a villain! He seemed such a very admirable person now – really a very exciting person indeed. Roger felt quite proud to know him! And yet he had been so scornful of him a short time ago. It just showed how careful you had to be in judging people.

They all spent a very busy and exciting day, but without much result. Rockingdown Manor was searched once more from top to bottom. Two men appeared from the grounds on the way over and joined them. They were the two men Roger had heard Mr King talking to the night before. They turned out to be men under him detailed to help him.

"Meet Jimmy and Frank," said Mr King, introducing them to the children. "The terrors of the police force – hunters of rogues and scoundrels and my very good friends!"

The children grinned. Jimmy and Fred were strong and well-built, but otherwise quite ordinary-looking except for their quick, observant eyes. They were both dressed in plain clothes.

"And Jimmy, Frank – meet Roger, Diana, Snubby and Loony," said Mr King. "Terrors too, all of them, especially this young lad, Snubby. Watch out for him, or he'll play one of his frightful tricks on you; he's a real pest. Actually, Loony is the best of the lot and quite the most intelligent."

This was the kind of foolery the children understood and liked. They laughed. They began to feel that things really must turn out all right if Jimmy, Frank and Mr King were all on the job. Barney would soon be back!

Down in the cellars at Rockingdown Manor Mr King looked at the rug and cushion on the wooden shelf. He also looked at the iron ring in the corner but, like the children, dismissed it as nothing. It did not occur to him to screw the great ring round and round.

"Nothing here," he said at last. "I think either Barney left the cellars and went up into the grounds and was captured or else the men came down here for some reason and found him. In any case he can't be anywhere near us, or he would yell and we would hear him."

Jimmy was sent to make inquiries about the boat, and Frank was sent to examine the iron gate barring the way to the underground stream. The children wanted to go too but Mr King said no – he didn't want a whole crowd of people about, in case the men got wind that something was up. Where they were he didn't know, but obviously they must be hidden somewhere about the countryside.

Jimmy came back and reported. "I've been to the farmhouse, sir. Said I wanted to buy some eggs. There was a boy there, in the boat, messing about on the backwater. He said the boat was his – he'd had it from his uncle for a present for his last birthday. Seemed quite honest, sir, I don't think there's any reason to disbelieve him."

"Well, there goes the mystery of the boat, then," said Mr King. "It belongs to a small boy who plays about in it! Ah, here's Frank. Perhaps he has something more interesting to report."

Frank hadn't. He had been to the iron gate and had done a lot of dragging away of greenery, pulling off enormous strands of ivy.

"No one has entered that way, sir," he reported. "It's impossible. Short of blasting out the gate with dynamite we'd never make an entry there. The solid earth has settled all round the gate, and it's absolutely immovable. I don't think that the stream has got much to do with this case."

Mr King rubbed his chin and frowned. "It's a real mystery, this," he said. "We know a mysterious aeroplane lands somewhere in that field, probably in the dry, flat area in the middle of it. We know a strange motor-launch haunts the spot where the stream joins the river. We suspect smuggling on a large scale here and yet we can't find out where the stuff goes, or how it comes out again from wherever its hiding-place is. And on top of all this a boy disappears into thin air – with a monkey – and we haven't the faintest notion where he's gone!"

"Do the men at the farmhouse know anything of this affair, do you think?" asked Roger.

"So far as we know, they don't," said Mr King. "The farm is run by an old farmer who has been there for years – man called Daws. His father had the farm before him, and they've a very good name. We've checked up on him all right and we've had a quiet inspection made of the whole farm, sent a man there who was apparently a livestock inspector, you know, and old Daws took him unsuspectingly around the farm, showing him every nook and cranny, most indignant that anyone should think he didn't keep on the right side of the law in every way!"

"Well, we really are at a dead end," said Roger. "There doesn't seem to be anything else we can do at all."

"I do wonder where Barney is," said Diana. "I keep thinking of him. What's he doing? I'm sure he must be very miserable and frightened."

"Barney's never really frightened," said Snubby. "He's one of these naturally brave people – he doesn't turn a hair when everybody else is shivering with fright."

All the same, Barney was not feeling very brave at the moment. He was not having a good time at all! He had spent the day before exploring everywhere, trying to find a way of escape, but without success.

As we know, he explored as far as the iron gate and gave that up. He discovered the rope hanging down from the hole in the rocky roof of the tunnel and gave that up too as a way of escape. The only thing left to do was to explore up the tunnel, and see where the stream came from. Maybe it flowed into the tunnel at a place where he could get out. On the other hand, of course, it might actually have its source underground, and not go into the open air at all until it poured out through the close bars of the iron gate. That really seemed rather more likely.

"Still, Miranda, we won't give up hope!" said Barney to the little monkey on his shoulder. "Come on, up the stream we'll go, but before that, what about finishing that ham and opening another tin of fruit?"

After a meal of ham and tinned pears the two of them set off up the stream instead of down. Barney came to the little passage that led to the shaft down which he had come the night before. He passed that, and went on up the stream, keeping to the little rocky ledge. Once the ledge stopped altogether and Barney had to leap to where it began again, hoping he wouldn't fall into the water and be soaked through!

He went on for fifteen minutes, flashing his torch round his feet to make sure of his next step. In places the ledge was slimy and slippery and he had to tread carefully. In other places the roof suddenly dipped down and he knocked his head against it before he realised it.

And then he came to a full stop. He couldn't go any farther. The roof had slanted down to the water, and there was no tunnel left – only a gurgling channel of water, hurrying through, pressing along, washing against the rock that completely hemmed it in. It was almost as if it were in a great pipe.

"Unless I get down into the water and make my way through it, completely submerged, head and all, I can't go any farther," thought Barney in despair. "And I daren't do that! I don't know how long the channel is before it becomes a tunnel again, with a ledge to walk on, and a roof above my head. I'd have to hold my breath under water for goodness knows how long, and probably I'd drown. As for Miranda, she wouldn't come at all. In any case she'd be swept away at once."

There was nothing for it but to go back the way he had come. He was very disappointed. When he came to the little slanting passage leading from the tunnel to the shaft he turned up it. He would climb up the shaft and get into that tiny little room above – he would have one more shot at moving that mysterious stone!

So up the passage he went with Miranda, and climbed the shaft to the top. He clambered out into the little room but no matter how he tried he could not make anything work that stone out of its place! He didn't know the secret, he didn't even know if the stone could be moved from this side. Probably it couldn't. Poor Barney, he really didn't know what to do next!

26

Miranda Gives the Game Away

Nobody came into the underground tunnel that day. Barney was there all alone with Miranda. He didn't like it at all, and wished hundreds of times that he had a watch. He had no idea whether it was twelve o'clock in the morning or six o'clock in the evening! Actually it was then about half past five in the afternoon. Outside it was broad daylight and bright sunshine. Down in the cave it was pitch dark unless Barney had his torch on.

He didn't like to keep it on too long in case the battery went. He knew how to turn on the big lights that flooded the cavern, but he was afraid of doing that in case the men came back unexpectedly and saw them. Then they would know that an intruder was there and hunt for him. Barney certainly didn't want to be discovered!

"What I want is to find a way of escape and go and tell the others all I've found out," thought Barney. "Then I suppose we'd have to go to the police – and what a surprise they would get!"

He had another meal, and Miranda ate some pineapple chunks from a tin and was extremely greedy over them. So was Barney. They both liked them very much. Then the boy went to stretch himself out on the mattress.

"This is very, very boring, Miranda," he told the monkey. "Gracious, are you still eating pineapple? You'll turn into a chunk if you don't look out! Miranda, what are we to do? Can't you think of something?"

Miranda chattered away, sucking at a bit of pineapple. She had got used to her strange surroundings now, and as long as she had Barney, and tinned peaches, pears and pineapple, she was quite prepared to stay in the tunnel for a long, long time.

"No books to read – nothing to do," groaned Barney, punching the pillow to fit his head. "It's frightful. There's only one thing to be said for this stay down here, Miranda, and that is I'm not spending any money! I've got precious little left, you know. We'll have to get a job soon, Miranda."

Miranda didn't mind that. She liked "jobs", especially when it meant showing off and having people clap and cheer her in the ring, or at a fair. That was grand!

Barney fell asleep about eight o'clock. He

slept for four or five hours and was then awakened by Miranda pulling at his ear and chattering.

He sat up, wondering where he was. He felt about for his torch and put it on. Of course, he was in that cavern, a prisoner who couldn't get out! He gazed round, wishing that he knew whether it was night or morning. It really was odd not to know.

"What's up, Miranda?" he said. "Stop grabbing my ear, silly!" But Miranda had heard something that Barney had not. She was warning him. He suddenly realised it, when he heard a heavy sound coming up the tunnel. He sprang to his feet.

The men were at work again. Then it must be the middle of the night – his second night there. They must be lowering stuff into the tunnel and soon some of them would be coming along to work the winches.

Barney knew he must hide. He decided to get behind the crates and spy on the men from there. He could hear their talk too. Taking Miranda on his shoulder he made his way to the side of the cavern where the big crates were stored, both full ones and empty ones. He found a place inside an empty crate. He could peer through the cracks.

Soon lights appeared down the tunnel and came nearer – the torches of the men walking up the tunnel. Then Barney heard their voices. There were five men this time. One or two were evidently foreigners, and spoke with a strange accent. Barney could barely understand what they said.

He gathered that more crates had arrived that night – dropped by an aeroplane somewhere not far off. Somehow they had been transported to the tunnel and were now about to be pulled up the stream by means of the wire rope wound up by the powerful winches.

And then Barney realised something he had not guessed before. The crates were not dragged up in the water just as they were but were apparently put on narrow, solid and very strong little rafts of wood. It was these rafts that the man with the pitchfork guided. The crates were heavy, the current was swift, and the rafts and crates bobbed about as they came up against the stream.

Barney watched breathlessly, peering through the crack in the empty crate. The men were soon hard at work, working the winches which whined and screeched, shouting to one another, pulling in the boxes and crates and cases as they appeared on their bobbing rafts. There were six of them.

Soon they were piled up with the others. Then one of the men, one of the chiefs or perhaps a foreman, gave an order. Two men manhandled a crate from the store and opened it.

It was full of bales of what looked like silk. Barney tried hard to see, but it was difficult. Then another crate was opened and Barney saw handguns being thrown out in a heap. A third crate was opened and the dull leaden-looking bars Barney had seen before, were flung out on the floor of the cave.

From another corner a man brought small boxes, and what looked like small canvas bags. The goods were rapidly packed in these. Barney guessed why. They could now be disposed of in small quantities here and there. They were thrown on to one of the bobbing rafts and the man with the pitchfork guided the raft down the stream, which soon disappeared from sight.

Another raft was loaded, and another. Then the men stopped work and had a meal. Barney hoped that they wouldn't discover that some of their tins were gone! They didn't. They opened a tin of chicken, a tin of meat and three tins of fruit. They found some bottles and opened those too, drinking from them without bothering about glasses or cups.

They opened more bottles and talked. It was difficult to hear what they said, and Barney could only catch a word now and again. They talked about horses and cars and food and the cinema, as far as he could tell.

Miranda, watching from Barney's shoulder,

saw one of the men toss an empty peach tin away. To Barney's horror she leaped from his shoulder, squeezed out of the crate and bounded over to the tin. She picked it up, chattering with pleasure because there was still some juice in it.

The man turned and saw her. His mouth fell open in amazement. He rubbed his eyes and looked again. Miranda was now licking out the tin.

"Hey, Joe," called the man. "Look here!"

Joe turned – and he too gaped in astonishment at the sight of Miranda. He got up at once.

"Look, you fellows, a monkey! Now where in the name of goodness did it come from?"

All the men gathered round Miranda. She looked up at them impudently. One of the men stroked her gently. In a second Miranda was on his shoulder, pulling his hair.

The men began to laugh. They gathered round the little monkey, teasing her, petting her, and even opened another tin for her.

"How did a monkey get here?" said Joe, in complete amazement. "We've never seen it before. Where did it come from? Surely it hasn't been here all the time."

"Course it hasn't. Don't be a fool, Joe," said a big man with a scar right down his face. "What I want to know is, did it come with anyone?"

Now it was Joe's turn to laugh. "That's a funny joke, that is! How would anyone get in here? There's only one way in and that's ours – and no one but us knows it."

"Well, how did the monkey get here then?" demanded the man with the scar.

"Oh, monkeys squeeze in anywhere," said Joe. "Artful little things, they are. Look at this one, eating a bit of peach just like you might – holding it in its hand and all!"

Barney watched Miranda, angry and afraid. Little idiot! She might give the whole game away now, betray the fact that he was there, in hiding.

She sat there, eating the peach, gradually getting very full indeed. In fact, she was now so full that she felt she could not eat the half peach that one of the men gave her as soon as she had finished the piece in her hand.

She suddenly thought of Barney. She would give him the peach. He liked peaches too! So she leaped away from the crowd of admiring men and went straight to the crate in which poor Barney was hiding! She disappeared inside, chattering.

"Is that its hiding-place?" said Joe, and went to peep at her, flashing his torch. Then he gave a tremendous shout:

"Hey, look here!"

The men came running up. They saw Barney crouching in an empty crate with

Miranda trying to push the peach in his mouth!

The men pulled him out roughly. "What are you doing here? How did you get here, into this tunnel? Go on, tell us everything or we'll make you very sorry for yourself!"

Barney looked round at the angry, glowering men. Now he was done for – silly little Miranda, her greed had made her give him away to the men. Joe shook him hard and Barney almost fell over.

"You tell us how you got in," said Joe, between his teeth. "Go on – quick!"

"All right," said Barney. "I'll show you. Let me go, I've not done any harm. I was only exploring a bit. Come on, I'll show you where I got in."

27

Miranda Does Her Best

Barney led the men up the tunnel, and then up the little passage to the shaft-hole. "I came down there," he said.

"Well, we know all about that old shaft," said the man with the scar. "It leads to a little stone room and that's all."

"Yes, but there's a moveable stone in the wall there that gives on to the old cellars of Rockingdown Manor," said Barney. "I moved the stone by accident when I was in the cellars and got through the gap. But the stone closed up again and I couldn't get back. So I came down the shaft and into the tunnel. I hid there. That's all."

"Anyone know anything about this moveable stone?" said the man with the scar, sharply, looking round at the men. They shook their heads.

"I'll go up with you," said the man, and he climbed up the shaft. Joe pushed Barney up behind him and then followed. "Go on up – you show him this wonderful stone!"

Barney showed the man the stone that moved. He looked over it carefully and then swung his torch all over the wall. He called to Joe to come up.

"Joe – see that stone? It's worked by a lever somewhere. Look for a little groove in the wall and a staple or something jutting out, almost unnoticeable. Destroy the mechanism. I'm not having anyone else find this secret way in!"

"So that's the explanation of this mysterious room," said Joe, elbowing Barney aside. "It must have been secretly built when the old house was first put up, two or three centuries ago – with a secret way in. What a nice quiet way of disposing of your enemies!"

"Very," said the man with the scar, in a dry voice that Barney didn't like at all. "Now get down the shaft, boy, and we'll decide how to dispose of you. Good heavens, is that monkey still on your shoulder?"

Back in the cavern the man questioned Barney carefully. When he heard that the boy was more or less a tramp, going from fair to fair and circus to circus, and had slept in the old house because he needed shelter, his face cleared a little.

"I see. Then you heard these noises, I suppose, and came down to explore and found the secret of the moving stone. Well, you seem a likely enough lad, the kind we

can train in our way of business – bit of
smuggling now and again. Like to join us?"

"No," said Barney.

That was quite the wrong thing to say.
The man was taken aback. He scowled at
Barney and then gave him a quick cuff on
the ear.

"Right! If that's the way you feel about
it, you can keep out. But you won't like it.

You'll be kept here till we can get you out, and then you'll be taken abroad and got rid of somewhere in a foreign land. We'll sell you to somebody who'll be glad of your help!"

"Anyway, he can work for us now," said Joe. "There's always plenty to do. The only difference is that he works for nothing because he's a fool, instead of working for good pay."

Barney felt his heart go cold. How long would the men keep him here, working underground for them? He felt sure they would not allow him to go up into the daylight with them. He would always be left behind here, in the dark, with only the sound of the stream for company.

"How long are you going to keep me here?" he asked, as boldly as he could.

"Maybe four weeks – maybe four months – it might even be four years," said the man with the scar, enjoying frightening the boy. "Depends how long our job goes on. You'll soon get quite fond of this place, won't you!"

Barney didn't think he would at all. He said nothing more. He was afraid of these rough-looking, scowling men, afraid they would treat him badly. He wasn't going to learn their illegal business but he could quite well see that he would have to turn to and do a lot of the dirty work for them, or else have a very bad time indeed. They would make as much use of him as they could.

Certainly the men made him keep hard at work that night! He had to help to guide the rafts up the stream, he had to help to take the crates and boxes to the side where they were stored, and he was given the job of undoing those that were to be sorted and repacked at once. He said nothing but did what he was told, though as slowly as he could.

His brain was working hard. How was he to escape? There must be some way. If only he could get a message to the others! They must be very worried about him by now. They would have gone down to the cellars to look for him and found his rug and cushion but nothing else to show where he had gone! They couldn't tell Miss Pepper and they certainly wouldn't tell Mr King.

Barney had been surprised that Mr King had not appeared underground with the men that night. Perhaps he directed operations from above ground. Well, if he came, Barney meant to tell him what he thought of him. What a fraud, what a hypocrite, what a humbug! Barney spent quite a lot of time thinking bad things for Mr King. Little did he know what different ideas the other children had of him now!

The men worked for several hours, and then went. They left Barney underground of course. "We'll be back tomorrow night," said Joe. "And you'll have to work hard again, so sleep for the day!"

"I don't know if it's day or night down here," said Barney, sullenly. "It's always pitch dark."

He spent a very miserable day indeed down in the darkness, switching on the big lamps at times to give him a change, though the men had forbidden him to do this. But he was not going to spend every hour in darkness. His torch was getting a little dim. He must save it.

He slept all the afternoon, though he did not know it was that time of day. He awoke about five o'clock and had a meal with Miranda. He had quite forgiven the little monkey for giving him away. He was very glad she was with him, to amuse him with her ridiculous little ways and to keep him company.

He felt very wide awake when he awoke, and wondered if it was night or morning. Perhaps it was morning as he felt so lively. He would have been surprised to know that it was getting on for evening!

He began to think of some way out of his difficulties. There simply must be some way. He looked at Miranda. She had found a pencil belonging to one of the men and was scribbling on a piece of paper taken from an empty packing case. She showed her scribbles to Barney, evidently thinking she had been very clever.

Barney pretended to read it: "'Please rescue us, we are in an underground tunnel.' Very clever, Miranda! Very clever indeed and beautiful writing."

He was just handing back the paper to her when a thought suddenly struck him. Miranda was used to taking notes or articles to people. Could she – could she possibly take a message from him to the others? She was a very tiny monkey – if she knew she was to go on a mission wouldn't she be able to find somewhere to squeeze through? She was so very small.

Barney had taught Miranda the trick of taking notes in the way that all good trainers teach their animals, by coaxing and reward. Many a time he had petted her and fondled her, and said someone's name over and over again, so that she would know where to take the note to, and when she had found that person and delivered the note, she had always been rewarded well by the one who received it.

Would she be able to find Snubby and take a note to him? Would she be able to squeeze out somewhere? It was worth trying even if nothing came of it.

Barney had a notebook in his pocket. He took it out and borrowed the pencil that Miranda was using.

He began to write. He told briefly what had happened to him and where he was. *How you can rescue me, I don't know,* he wrote. *I don't even know how you're to find the place in the roof where the men enter, dropping down on a rope. All I can say is it must be some place where there is a dip in the ground – some spot where the tunnel is very near the surface. Do what you can.*

When he had finished the note he folded it two or three times, took some thin string from his pocket and tied it up carefully. Then he felt about for Miranda's collar, which was buried in her thick neck-fur, and he tied the note firmly to it.

"Snubby," he said to the little monkey, fondling her. "Take it to Snubby. You know Snubby, don't you? Snubby, my friend who likes you so much. Take it to Snubby, to Snubby. Go find Snubby, Miranda, Snubby!"

Miranda listened, patting Barney's hands with her little brown paws. She knew quite well what he meant. She was to take the letter that Barney had put round her neck to his friend Snubby, the nice boy with the dog.

She leaped off Barney's shoulder and bounded over the rocky floor of the tunnel. Barney watched her. Where was she going? Did she know a way out? He couldn't believe that she did because she had not been away from him for even a minute!

Miranda went up the tunnel, not down. Barney was surprised. There is no way out there, Miranda! But in about twenty minutes she was back again, the note still on her collar. She had been up the shaft and into the little room at the top, remembering that that was the way they had come in, but of course there was no way out for her there, so after scrambling round for a while she had come back.

Barney petted her again. "Go on, find Snubby," he commanded. "You can find a way out if you try. Find Snubby, Miranda. It's very, very important!"

Miranda went off once more and this time she didn't come back. Barney wondered about her. Had she found a way out? If so, where was it? He was quite sure that if there was some hole or cranny through which she could squeeze she would certainly find it.

Miranda had remembered the other place she had been to with Barney, the iron gate. She had sensed the daylight on the other side, and now she remembered it. Snubby would be somewhere out in that daylight. She must find him.

She arrived at the barrier. More daylight came through now, because Frank had torn away so much of the overhanging greenery, and had pulled at the ivy that clung so thickly to the bars. Miranda climbed lightly up the gate. The bars were set very close indeed, too close even for Miranda to squeeze through. She tried her hardest. She almost got stuck in one place, and in her fright tore herself free so roughly that she made her leg bleed.

She sat down to lick it, chattering comfortably to herself. Then, feeling tired with her efforts she curled up in a corner and fell asleep. She slept for two or three hours and then awoke. She stretched herself and then felt the note on her collar. Ah, she must take it to Snubby. Barney had said so.

She looked consideringly at the barrier. She felt a little afraid of it since it had hurt her leg. She chattered rudely at the gate and then leaped on to it once more. She made a really good examination of it, from top to bottom, seeking for a way of escape.

And, at the bottom, she found a place where a bar had broken away at the surface of the water. Miranda got soaked as she squeezed through it. It was a tight fit, but she managed it! Now she was on the other side of the gate, in the dusk of the evening. Snubby! She must go and find Snubby. But which way was she to go?

28

An Exciting Night

The three children went to bed feeling down in the dumps that night. Even Mr King had confessed that he didn't know which way to turn. Barney really did seem to have vanished into thin air, and there appeared to be no more steps they could take either to find him or to clear up the mystery.

"I don't want to go to bed," said Diana. "I know I shan't go to sleep."

"Oh, yes you will," said Mr King firmly. "Off you go. It's ten o'clock already. Good gracious me, what would Miss Pepper say if she knew how late I have kept you up!"

They all went off, grumbling. Loony raced ahead of them. He never seemed to mind going to bed. He tore into Mr King's room, found his bedroom slippers, which were fleece-lined, and tossed them down the stairs. He then growled at all the rugs, dragged them into a heap where Mr King would be sure to fall over them, and left them there. Then he shot up the stairs as if a tiger were after him, landing on Snubby's bed in one last mad leap.

"Loony dog," said Snubby, who was taking off his socks. "Loony! Mad! Potty! Crazy!"

"Woof," said Loony happily, and flung himself on Snubby to lick every bit of him that he could.

Diana did fall asleep quickly, though she had felt certain she wouldn't. So did Roger. Snubby lay awake a little while and then slid off into a peculiar dream about Barney and Miranda.

He was awakened some time later by Loony. Snubby sat up in bed and felt for his torch. Where was it? The moon shone into the room through the trees, and gave a dim light, so he tried to see by that.

Loony was at the window, growling fiercely. He was on the window seat just inside the window and kept making darts at something outside, snapping and snarling.

"What's up, Loony?" said Snubby in surprise. He wondered if a burglar was trying to break into his bedroom. No, of course not, no burglar would face a growling dog like that!

Then something leaped right in through the window, sprang on to the top of a picture, and then up to the top of the curtain with a flying leap.

"Miranda! Oh, Miranda! It's you!" cried

Snubby, recognising the tiny creature as she leaped across a ray of moonlight. "Where's Barney?" Loony was now barking the place down, very angry to think that Miranda should dare to leap in at his master's window at night, when he, Loony, was on guard! Snubby threw a book at him. "Shut up, idiot! You'll wake the whole household. Shut up, I say!"

Loony subsided at last, and sprang on to the bed jealously. Miranda was now on the bar of the bed at the back. Snubby got out of bed and switched on the light, just as Diana and Roger, awakened by the noise, switched on theirs. Roger appeared sleepily at the door.

"Whatever's the matter with Loony? Has he gone mad or something?"

"No, look, Miranda's back!" cried Snubby, and at her name the little creature sprang to his shoulder, cuddling into his neck. Snubby put up his hand to pet her, and at once felt the note tied to her collar.

"I say – what's this? A note! I bet it's from Barney!" he cried. He took off the note and undid the string round it. He opened it out. Roger came to read it with him, and Diana too, eager to join in the excitement.

"Well!" said Snubby, when they had all finished reading it. "Fancy all this happening to Barney. Gosh, what a pity nobody can get that stone down in the cellars to move now. Fancy that Barney's down underground where the river is. Would you believe it?"

"We'll have to rescue him somehow," said Diana at once. "I say, won't Mr King be thrilled to hear of this!"

"Better go and tell him," said Roger, and all three went racing down the stairs, bursting into Mr King's room after a very quick knock. He was asleep.

But he woke up completely as soon as he read Barney's note. "My word! This is news! So that's where the goods go to – where Barney is now. In some cavern underground, reached by way of the stream in the tunnel. But how can we find where that hole in the roof is, the one the men use to drop the goods down? I see it all now . . . the only missing link is the bit where the hole in the roof is. We've got to find that, and all is clear!"

"Can we do something about it tonight?" asked Snubby, excited.

"I can – but you're not going to," said Mr King firmly, to the bitter disappointment of all three children. He got out of bed and went down to the telephone. Frank and Jimmy and two other men were told to come along to Rockingdown Cottage. "Things are moving!" said Mr King.

He shooed the children away and dressed. He was ready by the time the other men came. The children said goodbye so meekly that Mr King ought to have guessed they had something up their sleeves – but he didn't.

Under their dressing-gowns the children were fully dressed! They meant to follow Mr King and the four men, and to "see the fun", as Snubby put it.

Before he went off with his men, Mr King took a long look at a map he had. He put his finger on a certain spot. "We know that the hole in the roof of the river-tunnel is in some place where the ground dips considerably," he said. "That means a hollow somewhere, and there's only one place where there is a hollow on Rockingdown Hill, and that's where the farmhouse is built that you went to the other day, Jimmy."

"Right," said Jimmy. "That's it! The job is worked from there. Old Daws doesn't know anything about it, of course, he's too old. It's all done under his nose and he doesn't suspect a thing! I reckon it's that son-in-law of his who's in with the gang. He's a nasty piece of work."

"Well, we're going there now," said Mr King. "We'll be quite a surprise-party! We might even catch them red-handed. But if they're not there we've got to find that hole in the tunnel roof and do a little dropping in ourselves. Well, children, we'll see you in the morning!"

They said goodbye to the three children and strode off into the night. "We needn't hurry," said Roger to Snubby, seeing him begin energetically to strip off his dressing-gown. "We know where they're going. We mustn't follow too close behind in case they spot us and send us back. We'll go in about five minutes' time."

So they waited, very impatiently, for about five minutes, and then, with Loony at their heels, they set off. Miranda had gone again, though nobody saw her. They looked for her and came to the conclusion that she must have gone back to Barney.

They knew the way to the farm well now, and picked the best route they could. Once they got to the little backwater that led to the pond in the farmyard they knew they were getting very near. They crept alongside the water and came to the pond.

"Look – do look – that must be Mr King and his men, hunting everywhere with torches," said Snubby in a whisper. "They haven't woken anybody at the farm yet. Funny the dogs aren't barking."

"Let's hide somewhere safe," said Roger. "Look, here's an old barn. We'll go in there and hide in some straw."

They went into the old barn. A great heap of manure was in one corner. A pile of straw was in another. The children slipped into the straw and pulled it over them. They could wait there till things boiled up a bit, then they would creep out and see what was happening. The moonlight slanted into the barn and filled the place with light and with black shadows. It was all very exciting.

Loony was as quiet as a mouse. Snubby's hand was on his collar. "I simply can't think why the farm dogs don't bark," began Snubby in a whisper. "What's happened to them?"

"Don't know; either somebody's keeping them quiet, for some reason, or they're not here," said Roger, also puzzled.

His first idea was right. The farm dogs were being kept quiet by someone who had spotted Mr King and his men, someone who wanted the others to escape before the dogs barked, when he would have to come out into the open, and answer Mr King's awkward questions!

Suddenly the barn door was pushed slowly and softly open. Roger saw it and clutched Snubby and Diana, whispering into their ears. "Look, someone's coming in. Keep Loony quiet."

A man came in, silently, and slunk over to the manure heap. Another followed and another, a whole line of them. Who were they? Where had they come from? The children had no idea. Loony stiffened and the fur on his neck rose up, but he made no sound.

Roger regretted bitterly that he had come into the barn with the others to hide. There might be a fight in here, when Mr King and his men came seeking with their torches – and somebody might get hurt.

He peered out of the straw. The men had pitchforks and were moving the manure heap rapidly. Then one knelt down and loosened something in the floor. He took out what looked like boards. Then he swung himself down and disappeared. All the men followed him save one. He stood there alone, panting as he pitchforked the manure back into place.

The children watched silently, their hearts beating fast. The hole in the roof of the tunnel! Why, it was here, in the floor of the barn, just a little way away from them. The men had gone down into the tunnel – the river must flow directly under this old barn. It probably fed the pond and the backwater in some way, as well as going on and on down to the iron gate.

The man who was left threw down his pitchfork on the manure and crept to the door. He went out and disappeared. A minute or two later the dogs of the farm began to yelp madly, and a voice called out sharply.

"Who's there! Come out and show yourselves. What are you doing on my farm at night?"

Then Mr King's voice answered sternly, and there was quite a meeting in the middle of the farmyard. The old farmer did not appear. He was sound asleep. It was the son-in-law who did all the talking.

"What nonsense! I know nothing about smuggled goods – nothing about entrances to underground rivers. You must be mad. Haven't the police anything better to do than look for things that aren't there and never have been? I tell you, you can go all over the place from top to bottom and you'll find nothing suspicious at all!"

Roger suddenly flung aside the straw in

which he was hiding and ran to the door. Mr King might be wild with him for coming here, when he had forbidden him, but he had to say what he knew. He shouted at the top of his voice:

"Mr King! Mr King! We know where the hole is. It's in here, in the barn. And a lot of men have just escaped down it, waiting for you to go; then they'll come out again."

There was an astonished silence. "Well, you little pest! You've come after all, and the others too, I suppose," said Mr King. He strode over to the barn with his men. Roger pointed to the heap of manure. "It's under there. You'd never have guessed. Move it aside and you'll see! Gosh – isn't this exciting!"

29

The End of it All

Barney was in the cavern when Miranda came back without the note. He petted her, very pleased. He gave her a big piece of pineapple from a tin as a reward. Now the others knew where he was, they would think of a way to rescue him.

And then things began to happen very quickly indeed. The men arrived in a hurry, strangely silent. They didn't work the winches. They brought no rafts with cases on them. They clustered together in the cavern, their faces anxious. They seemed to have forgotten all about Barney.

He didn't like the look of them. Supposing they had been driven underground because Roger had got on to the police, and they had got wind of it? They might guess that Barney had something to do with it, and might turn on him. He decided it would be a very, very good thing to hide.

But where? Not in the empty crates, they would think of that at once. He would climb up the rocky wall of the cavern at the back and find a ledge to lie on. Barney silently crept away right to the back of the vast cavern and made his way up the wall, carefully feeling for jutting-out bits to hold on to with his hands and feet, climbing up bit by bit.

He found a very narrow ledge, so narrow that he almost rolled off it if he took a deep breath. But it was hidden from down below. He lay there with Miranda, listening.

And now came other voices, shouting and calling commands. Barney could hear Mr King's loudest of all, and was astonished. Mr King! Had he come down to be with the other men too then? Barney had no idea that the tutor had nothing to do with the men. He was amazed to hear all that Mr King shouted.

"You may as well give in! We're armed, and we know all about you. Either you surrender now, or we seal up the hole in the roof and leave you to starve."

"We won't surrender," Barney heard Joe say to the others. "We've got plenty of food here. We shan't starve."

"And how long will that last us?" said the man with the scar. "A week at the most. Don't be a fool, Joe. We're caught here like rats in a trap. Why did we ever come down? If we had thought for one moment we'd have known that we had done for ourselves as soon as we came down here!"

They talked again, heatedly, urgently, some for surrender, some for staying down. Mr King shouted again.

"I'll give you five minutes. Stay down if you like, while we get hold of your chief up here – yes we know all about him – and he'll talk all right to save his own skin. He's talked before, you know. We'll come and collect you when you want to be collected. A little starvation diet won't do you any harm."

"I'm giving up," said the man with the scar. "It won't do us any good to try to shoot it out, or to refuse to surrender. You all know we're caught. We've had a good run for our money. Well, I'm off to surrender. Anyone coming with me?"

"What about that boy?" said Joe suddenly. "Can't we do a bit of bargaining over him? Can't we say we'll keep him down here with us and starve him to death?"

"I'd forgotten about him!" said the man with a scar. "Where is he? Find him."

But they couldn't find him. They didn't see him lying precariously on a high ledge at the back, trying not to breathe.

"Well," came Mr King's stentorian voice, "your time is up. We're getting out and the hole will be sealed up. A man will be on guard in the barn. Knock three times on the boards if you want to surrender."

Then the men got panic-stricken. They surged towards the tunnel, forgetting Barney.

"We'll give in!" shouted Joe. "You've got the upper hand, and we know it all right. We're coming."

"One at a time, round the corner of the tunnel," came the directions. "Hands up as you come, or we fire."

So, one at a time, round the corner of the tunnel went the men, holding their hands as high as they could, stumbling over the rocky ledge. And one by one they were hauled up the hole, and had handcuffs neatly clicked on their wrists as soon as they were in the barn. Jimmy and Frank greeted one or two of them by name.

"Well, if it isn't Joe! You just can't stay out of trouble, can you, Joe? And here's Frisky again, large as life and twice as ugly – to think you're in this racket too! And who would have thought of meeting you here, Scarface?"

The last man was out. Mr King spoke sharply to him. "Where's the boy who had the monkey? If you've harmed him things will go hard with you."

"I don't know where he is," said the man sullenly. "He's not there. We looked for him."

Roger could keep quiet no longer. He went to the hole and peered down it. "Barney! Barney! Miranda! Come along,

we're all here. Everything's safe."

Barney was already coming along the tunnel. He had watched the last man go, and reckoned it was safe for him to appear again. He heard Roger's yell and yelled back:

"I'm coming! I'm coming!"

He was hauled up. The three children and Loony fell on him and almost suffocated him. They were overjoyed to see him.

"We got your note! Miranda brought it!"

"The hole in the roof was under a manure heap in this old barn!"

"Are you all right? Are you hungry?"

The handcuffed men eyed the children in amazement. Where had they sprung from in the middle of the night? How very extraordinary. The chief, who had sent the men down into the hole and covered up the boards with manure, looked sullen and downcast. He was the old man's son-in-law, and under cover of getting in men to help on the farm and do repair work, he had brought in these villains, persuading them to help him in his illegal doings.

"And now," said Mr King, looking quite sternly at the four children, "it's really time you behaved like children and got yourselves to bed. Barney, I'm glad to see you safe, but you've had a very narrow escape, I think. As for you others, how you dared to follow me after I'd said you were not to come amazes me – and if you hadn't unexpectedly been of the very greatest help, I should have a lot more to say about disobedience. But as things are I shall probably not say anything."

He grinned suddenly, and the children grinned too. Good old Mr King!

"I suppose we can't stay any longer then?" said Roger.

"Not one moment," said Mr King. "And this time I expect complete obedience to my orders. Get back home and get into bed. I'll see you in the morning. I've got to stay here and see this little lot safely put away for the night!"

Barney, Roger, Diana, Snubby, with Miranda and Loony, took a last look at the sullen men and then stumbled back home. Snubby yawning loudly, and setting everyone else off too. Then he sneezed.

"Oh dear, don't say you've caught cold," said Diana in alarm. Snubby's colds were awful, and he sniffed dreadfully.

"No, just pepper up my nose," said Snubby, yawning again. "Oh my, what will Miss Pepper say – and Roundy – when they hear what we've been up to!"

They all got to bed eventually. Barney was given one of the spare-room beds and cuddled down into it with Miranda, marvelling at its softness.

In the morning they could hardly believe

all the happenings of the night before. Barney was thrilled to wake up and find himself in the cottage instead of in the dark cavern. There was such a tremendous chattering upstairs that Mrs Round came up to see what was the matter as soon as she arrived.

She listened, open-mouthed. She couldn't say anything at all except, "Well I never – you youngsters! Well I never!"

When Mr King arrived in time for breakfast she regarded him with the greatest of awe. She cooked him a very special breakfast of ham and eggs. She never once took her eyes off him, even backing out of the room so that she could look at him till the last moment.

"What in the world have you told Mrs Round?" said Mr King, half irritated. He looked tired but pleased. He tucked into his breakfast eagerly.

The children finished their own breakfast, which was not quite so special as Mr King's, and waited patiently for him to push away his plate and finish his coffee.

"Well, it's all tied up nicely," he said. "Very, very nicely. Tanner, the son-in-law of the old farmer, and incidentally a very bad lot, has spilled the beans – in other words he's told us everything. It has saved us quite a bit of trouble. I'm afraid, however, he'll get into a spot of trouble himself when he's out of prison, because the others won't easily forget how he betrayed them!"

"Serve him right," said Snubby, who hated disloyalty.

"It was a very pretty little plot," said Mr King. "All kinds of goods were flown here from different countries. The aeroplane touched down in that field you know of, threw out the goods and made off again. The cases were manhandled to the stream and put on the little rafts Barney has probably told you about. They were pulled upstream by two men rowing the little unnamed boat that presumably belonged to the farmer's boy."

"In the dark, I suppose?" said Roger.

"Oh yes, always at night," said Mr King. "They were then manhandled again to the barn and dropped down the hole into the water – the rafts were dropped first, of course, and it wasn't very difficult to arrange the cases safely on the rafts, tie them to the wire rope, and then wind them up to the cavern by means of the winches. Once there, the cases were perfectly safe and could be unpacked, and the goods sorted and repacked in small packets and bags, ready for sale secretly."

"They must have made a lot of money," said Roger.

"They did," said Mr King. "They made just a few mistakes, though. They hired an electric launch which came slinking up the river to collect all these small packages and parcels, and they didn't pay the owner what they owed him, so he talked a bit and his talk came round to us. That was what really made us suspect there was something going on, on a rather big scale."

"What other mistakes did they make?" asked Roger.

"Well, they didn't realise that thuds and bangs underground are often magnified when a building stands overhead," said Mr King. "Though even if they did realise it they would probably think that as the house was empty, nobody would hear them. But the biggest mistake of all was that they didn't realise there were four tiresome children, to say nothing of a monkey and a dog, who were going to suspect their poor old tutor, and snoop round him and his doings, and fall headlong into the mystery themselves! Aha – that was a very big mistake indeed!"

They all laughed, and Loony tugged madly at Mr King's shoelaces. "No good, Loony," said Mr King. "They're special ones, made of leather, quite unchewable."

"What will Miss Pepper say?" said Diana. "She's coming back today!"

Once she had recovered from her amazement, Miss Pepper said rather a lot. She rounded on Mr King for deceiving her regarding his ability to teach. "All those wonderful references!" she said. "I'm shocked, Mr King."

"Don't be," said Mr King. "These kids have learned a lot since I've been here. As for the references, they were all true – I did do some tutoring before I took up my present job. Cheer up, Miss Pepper, at least you weren't here when all this blew up."

"I should have been," said Miss Pepper. "It is scandalous that all this should happen when I was away."

"Yes. We ought to have waited till you came back," said Mr King, and that made everyone laugh.

"Well, I'm glad it's all cleared up happily," said Miss Pepper. "What a tale! What will their parents say?"

"You don't need to bother about that," said Mr King. "I'm going to see them when they come back, and tell them everything myself. I can assure you that they will not blame you for anything, Miss Pepper."

"I can't stay on at the cottage after all this," said Miss Pepper. "Not that I meant to, anyhow, because I'm taking my sister away to the sea and I mean to take the children too. It will be so much nicer for them – swimming, sailing, fishing – much more to do than there is here."

This was great news. The children were thrilled.

"What about Barney? Can he come too?" Snubby asked.

"Well, there isn't really room, but I dare say we can squeeze him in," said Miss Pepper. "He certainly seems one of us now."

But Barney shook his head. "No, thank you," he said. "I've got a job. I'm joining a fair tomorrow – it's on its way through Rockingdown Village today. I met someone I knew who told me about it when I went to the village for Mrs Round this morning. It's time Miranda and I earned our living again!"

This was disappointing, very, very disappointing. They would miss Barney terribly. Would they ever see him again? Would he find his father some day? Now they would never know!

But when the children heard that the fair was actually coming to the seaside place where Miss Pepper was taking them, in ten days' time, they cheered up. They would see Barney then!

"And I also must say goodbye," said Mr King. "I have my living to earn as well – but not as a tutor, I am thankful to say. I must get back to headquarters and forget this pleasant little interlude with children and monkeys and dogs!"

"Only one monkey and one dog," said Snubby.

"And quite enough," said Mr King, pushing Miranda off his shoulder and Loony off his feet. He stood up. "I'm saying goodbye now. You were my bitter enemies at first but I hope we're friends now!"

"Oh, yes," said everyone, and then he was hugged by Diana, and thumped on the back by the boys, while Loony barked madly.

Barney went down the front path with him, having said goodbye too. The children watched them go, feeling rather sad that such a wonderful adventure had come to an end.

"All the same, I feel that we'll have more adventures with Barney and Miranda some day," said Snubby, picking Loony up and squashing him till he squealed. "I feel it in my bones."

And I shouldn't be surprised if he's right!